LITTLE MISS COCKTAIL

David Lozada

For my best friend, James.

Table of Contents

Chapter 1 - Triple Penetration...7

Chapter 2 - My Blumpkin...15

Chapter 3 - The Third Nipple...29

Chapter 4 - Wimpy Hut Jr...53

Chapter 5 - Party Time...61

Chapter 6 - Yachts 'N Thots...81

Chapter 7 - 864 Mesmerizing Inches...93

Chapter 8 - Soggy Biscuit...119

Chapter 9 - Dickbutt...133

Chapter 10 - Toilet...147

Chapter 11 - Psycho...163

Chapter 12 - Chicken Noodle Soup...167

Chapter 13 - Mom's Spaghetti...187

Chapter 14 - Inner Demons...203

Chapter 15 - The Morning After...209

ABOUT THE AUTHOR...213

Chapter 1
Triple Penetration

The vast red sky materialized in an array of checkered patterns, not unlike the foreskin of the pissing cadet beneath it.

His yellow water took on the shape of the shitty gray ground and introduced color to an otherwise monotone landscape. The pale city's plan seemed random and haphazard, like the strange placement of pubic hair. Despite this, the setting never ceased to be familiar.

Upon his last spurt of triumph, he wiggled his worm in an attempt to summon the remaining juices within. As a cocktail of pee neared his dickhole, a shot rang out from afar.

The piss pool's surface was breached by the severed balls of the former cadet.

The newest acolyte of impotency fell backward. His body splashed on the yellow earth loudly.

A pair of sexy blue eyes above scanned the area. Two lovely lips parted.

"Nice job Siss. Let's get a move on."

Two dark figures jumped from one building rooftop to the next, abruptly ending at a ledge. Despite the thickness of circumstance, the air felt light, as if it wasn't there.

The puffy pink rims welcomed the tube of a silver liquor flask. A woman's scintillating sights detected another loner below.

"Four blocks down. Touching himself. Take care of it."

Another tin glinted in the darkness as a cord of red hair fell upon the shaft of a sniper rifle. The careful fingering of the gun's G spot elicited a satisfying bang.

A freshly beheaded corpse deflated onto the broken pavement.

"Keep up the pace."

More jumping. The scarlet grinned with arousal from all the foreplay.

A pair of slick boots ground to a halt, followed by the clacking of seductive heels behind them. The noise attracted the attention of a few military voyeurs who emerged from the dark of the concrete masses.

"Sissy, more uniforms, but you're gonna have to—"

Cracks beneath them splintered like veins.

"Shit. Just come—"

The rooftop gave way and the girls fell through. The scarlet's grin mutated to full-on laughter.

"You gotta slow down Chrissy. I haven't moistened up yet!"

The pair's landing boomed across a foreboding black room. A spotlight switched on to reveal the fresh new meat.

The first was a bodacious blonde wearing a garrison cap. Her dark green outfit buttoned up to a point where just the right amount of cleavage was shown. Her brass and silky platforms shone bright in the light.

Behind her stood another feline of short black mane, also wearing a cap. Dressed in similar garb to the girl in front of her, this lady substituted her lack of a decent bust size with two sensuously smooth legs. She warmed her throat with warm liquor from a can and spoke.

"You know what she meant bitch. Hurry the hell up."

"Missy, you of all people should know that jerking off is a delicate process. You gotta be gentle with your clit!"

The second girl turned to the first, shaking her head back and forth. "Chrissy, I just... I just can't."

"Nevermind her, she'll be here any second. Focus on what's in front of us." The leader's blue diamonds squinted. "This isn't even close to being over."

Multiple spotlights juiced up and peered downward, revealing an orgy of uniforms poised with assault guns. As more lamps ignited, the possibility of casual intercourse grew less firm. A thorough chafing became inevitable.

The blonde lifted her fists and arched her back.

"Looks like we get to throw down after all. Missy, you ready?"

In a swift motion, two sabers materialized in the ravager's hands. She tilted her head with rascal charm.

"Way ahead of you."

The swordswoman lunged forward, soaring meters in seconds. Before the first bum could unload his package, a shiny blade cut his ass in two.

Her sabers danced in the limelight, penetrating deep into every victim. The trail of bodies was excellent evidence of the warrior's proficient hand labor.

The blonde chick leaped into the air with full force, pushing effortlessly against gravity's weak pull. She descended flawlessly into a group of soldiers, squeezing her landing's head against the floor. His cranium sank deeper and deeper and deeper until his intelligence finally popped.

With the swing of a thigh she knocked a pair way back, then managed to punch a dude right in his balls. She was more than capable of going in raw.

Grunts and squeals resounded rhythmically as steel and fists moved in and out of the light. Despite the beating, the pack didn't seem to be receding. If anything, it was only growing larger.

A saber sliced a limb while a martial arts move cracked another. Though the girls were rowdy now, they knew their drive wouldn't last forever.

At the disconnection of a ball from a socket, some dick way back ejaculated way into the air, then came crashing down in a red blur. His body spinning every which way upon impact, a pair of 9mm firearms on top began spraying away.

A smile between two pigtails grew more wholesome with every pull. Assholes all around felt the full push of a bullet deep inside them. In a matter of seconds, the majority of the horde's nutter had been buttered.

The spinning sausage came to a stop. What was left of his physical features laid in a colorful bed around his cadaver. A young, petite redhead straddled the mess.

Dressed similarly to the two girls before her, she was noticeably smaller. Though she had the smallest curves, she showed the most skin, giving fans what they want but keeping them around for a little more.

A survivor cowered in fear a few feet ahead, tears streaming from both his eyes and his penis. The femme fatale raised a cannon.

"Do ya feel lucky punk?"

The wet one stared, mouth agape.

"Well, do ya?"

As he began to swing his head, a bullet gave him the pleasure of his last fellatio. The two other girls appeared.

The short-haired girl crossed her arms. "It's always gotta be a show with you, huh?"

"I've been told I put on quite the performance." The scarlet's pigtails bounced as she gave a cute wink. "Not that you would know anything about that."

"Listen, bitch, why don't you just shut the—"

"Enough!" The blonde stepped in, shaking her head with a smirk. "Won't you two ever get along?"

"Well… not until Missy gets laid."

The swordfighter made a blank face and spoke to the ceiling. "God… why me?"

After a pause, the redhead leaned in. "At least I don't have hepatitis!"

"What the fuck—"

"Girls!" The voluptuous vixens faced their leader. "Stop bickering and focus. This isn't a game we're playing here."

An echo filled the space. Something of weight had arrived.

"Girls! Ready up!"

Rapiers and M&P 9s sprang out of the girls' hands. Footsteps banged loudly against the floor, intensifying as they approached the circle of the spotlight.

"You two fall back." The blonde smirked. "I've got first try."

Her teammates vanished. The footsteps stopped.

"Hey handsome." The boss lady's seductive voice had a tinge of mockery in it. "Don't be shy."

A tremendous form came into the light. He appeared to be the general of the wasted troops strewn around him, as his chest carried medals of sumptuous honor. This last encounter ventured closer, stopping to stand fully erect mere meters from the well-lipped beauty.

She looked up at the brute with her piercing gaze, sassily putting a hand on her hip. His size did not impress.

"You look like the type of guy who doesn't last long with a woman."

He threw a punch, attempting to fist her. With little effort, she caught his thrust and, after a smirk of pity, sent him flying across the room.

Flabbergasted by his shittiness, the general pushed himself up slowly. About halfway, he turned abruptly and lunged.

His ankle was caught in midair by a flexible band of chain. Once again, his pansy ass went soaring.

The links wrapped around the arm of the cropped belle. She extended one hand and made a tiny gap between two fingers.

"Looks like you're a bit too small for this fight."

The general managed to muster some shred of dignity to get up, yet couldn't help but look like he greatly underperformed. A cloud of smoke spewed behind him.

The last goddess rode a robust missile headed straight toward its target. The juiced-out enemy knew in that instant that this fight had prematurely ended.

The redhead's tendrils flapped in the air as she uttered a final farewell to the general.

"Fucking bye!"

She pushed off her partner and the bombshell ignited in the loser's face with a flourish of high impact sexual violence.

The explosion's clouds filled the scene and through a strange transition, the whiteness of everything quickly faded to black.

Chapter 2
My Blumpkin

A slightly used condom reflected the waning summertime as Val scuffled down a weedy sidewalk. The emasculated heat evaporated from the surface of its complex latex construction.

The plainly dressed brunette had her first bartender interview today smack dab in the middle of West Bubblefuck. The dried contraceptive fluttered in the mid-afternoon breeze.

As her cheap ballerina shoes ambled toward their destination, thoughts of trepidation leaked into the girl's mind.

This was an opportunity that couldn't get creamed.

Val looked down at her smartphone that was, at best, retro or, at worst, prehistoric. The place was just around the bend.

Nervousness kissed every inch of her body as she bumbled forward. Her tummy started grumbling again, but she told herself she would eat after. Behind her, the city's skyline reared its delusions of grandeur.

The candidate neared the hole of entry, the likes of which was surrounded by a thick, untrimmed bush. This bar looked like a rundown shack, as if feces glued its toilet pieces together. But Val had no other choice.

This was to be her glory hole.

The door to Shitdom suddenly opened. Out came a sublime female of pixie-cut beauty. Her rose-colored blouse matched nicely with her fitted black skirt. She smelled like fresh tobacco and booze. A yellow mark stained her collar.

The girl pulled out a lighter and a cigarette. She glanced at the orifice in front of her and leaned against the shack to ignite. She gave off a very fuck-you attitude, but Val didn't give it much thought.

"Um… e-excuse me?"

She was far too busy being a pussy anyway. Summoning the assertiveness of her non-existent testes, she tried again.

"E-Excuse me?"

After a long drag and an exhalation, the pixie-haired girl loosened her lips.

"Just go in already."

"Wha—"

"I said go in, you bumfuck." Oh, she was quite the snarky one. "You're looking for a job right? Go in already, for fuck's sake."

"I, uh… well OK I guess. T-Thank you."

The other woman kept satisfying her oral fixation, looking at the city unravel. Val passed through the doorway.

"Don't get your hopes up kid."

The bitch said that with a smile, but Val didn't notice. Shaking off her fear, she inserted herself into the cabin.

Val could barely see through the thick, dank haze. Before she could walk five steps over to the flickering computer monitor in the right corner of the room, the innocent child felt herself becoming contact high.

The machine spoke to her.

"Good afternoon. Would you happen to be Valorie?"

Cannabis clouds swirled around her head. Val's eyes were fiery red now. She had been in the room for about 10 seconds. It usually takes her five to become completely stoned.

"Hey baby."

She plopped atop the computer desk and leaned in close to the monitor's speakers. "I've got something special for you, my blumpkin."

"Excuse me, Valorie?"

She twirled off, badly singing Korean pop anthems as she cranked her ass slowly to the beat.

"Oh, oh, oh, oh, sexy lady."

The monitor blared. "Missy! Did you smoke weed inside the house again?!"

The girl outside chuckled. Val continued shaking her ass.

A door in the room popped open. A lioness sprang forth with golden mane so bright a hotel heiress would orgasm. She somehow kept her composure amid the injustice that was Val's twerking.

It took Val a little while to notice that her interviewer had arrived. She ceased her 'dancing' with flat buttocks in midair.

The two stared at each other, each perplexed at the other's existence. Val sank to a low crouch, as if threatening to pee if anyone said a word.

The blonde broke the strange, highly uncomfortable silence. She cleared her throat and spoke with a smile.

"It's a pleasure to meet you, Valorie. My name's Chrissy, and I'll be your interviewer."

She extended her arm. Val looked at it suspiciously, then moved her hand to complete the handshake. Somehow, she missed her target and fell face-first into the floor.

***

Though Val's head was still spinning when she awoke, she had thankfully lost the urge to shake her ass.

Beige wallpaper peeled away from the small room she found herself in. Empty bottles of booze and yellowish stains decorated the edges of the space. She got up slowly from the pillow and blanket she lay under and walked over to a table with four empty seats.

The spot closest to her had a steaming plate of chicken, mashed potatoes and green peas. Her stomach bellowed, reminding her that it'd been a while since she last ate.

"Bee-bee-boo-bop!"

Val could hear someone from the next room. She stood up straight, trying hard to forget how badly she had embarrassed herself.

"Bee-bee-boo-beep!"

A scarlet vixen with hair tied into pigtails emerged. She had on the same red and black uniform as the chick from before, but wore her skirt significantly higher.

Her face lit up. "What up girl?!"

Was this girl high too?

"Ermm... hello?"

The girl glared at Val unnaturally, as if she had just injected four marijuanas.

The door opened again and the smoker from before walked in, still dressed in uniform. Without looking at the other two, she walked over to the only spot on the table with food and sat down. She grabbed a fork and started eating like an animal on the brink of starvation.

Another familiar body entered the room. The conditioner-imbued blonde beamed a smile at Val as she gracefully entered.

"Hi again Valorie! So sorry about before. We've been having problems with our ventilation lately."

Chrissy shot a disapproving look at the girl feasting. Missy kept munching away.

"Sorry about the mess in here, too. Please have a seat! It's the least we can do. You must be hungry after your nap anyway."

Val tried hard not to blush. "Oh, t-thank you Miss—"

"Chrissy! Just call me Chrissy."

"R-Right. Thank you, Chrissy, but it's OK if we just have our interview. I can just go grab something after—"

"No way! We made you a plate anyway. We'll do the interview afterward. Sissy?"

Val hadn't noticed that the redhead was staring at her this entire time.

"Can you get Miss Valorie her plate in the kitchen?"

"Yessir!"

Sissy merrily bounced into the room she came from. Chrissy pointed to the seat across from her—the one right next to Missy.

"Please have a seat!"

Val could feel a bead of sweat roll down the side of her face. What did she get herself into?

"T-Thank you. You're very kind."

"Stop thanking me. You're our guest!"

Missy looked annoyed as Val took the seat next to her. With a mouth full of meat she sprayed, "Chrissy, why are we even bothering? She's a fucking pansy ass."

The blonde sighed. "Missy, would you please just—"

"I mean we've got a handle on everything ourselves. Plus we don't have to risk things going to shit like with—"

"That's enough, Missy. Shut up and eat your food."

The short-haired girl looked down at her plate with a frown. "Yeah, alright. Sorry." She resumed eating.

Sissy rolled in with two plates and set them in front of Chrissy and Val. Before she went back into the kitchen to grab her own, she twisted around and started twerking.

"Hey new girl! Am I doing it right?"

Missy giggled as Val's face turned bright red. Chrissy was unamused.

"Sissy, go grab your damn plate and sit your ass down."

"L-O-L alright, alright, I was just teasin' ya." She winked.

Val tried to hide her face by staring down at her plate. When pigtails returned, Chrissy spoke again.

"Sorry about my girls. They can be quite… rambunctious."

Missy chimed in. "You don't have to be so embarrassed. Sissy shakes her ass for money in her spare time."

The scarlet happily replied, "It beats sucking dick all day!"

"I will sever your urethra."

"Bring it!"

"Girls! Are you serious right now?!"

Chrissy's bark reverberated through the room. Her two employees hung their heads in penance.

The leader cleared her throat and grinned at Val. "Never a boring day around here!"

Val forced a smile back at her, but couldn't help shake the feeling that this job opportunity was far from normal.

Her stomach cried out again.

"Oh, you must be hungry! Please dig in!"

Val's mouth began to water as the smell of roasted meat filled her nostrils. She felt like she shouldn't take a bite, but the pain in her gut was too strong to resist.

"O-OK. Thank you very much."

She picked up her fork and knife, cut a piece of the chicken and placed it in her mouth. She could feel her entire body tingle as she chewed her meal. Val hadn't eaten anything outside of pasta, crackers and ramen noodles for several months.

She tried hard to avoid being consumed by ecstasy. In between a bite, Chrissy asked her a question.

"So, do you live in the city?"

Val thought about how far behind she was on rent. "Yes ma'am. I live downtown."

"Downtown, nice! We hit a lot of bars in that area. Great crowd!"

The candidate tried to figure out what she meant by that. Was this some kind of on-demand bartender temp agency?

Val continued speaking. "Yeah, so I'm pretty familiar with all the bars and venues there. I've even worked at a few during training."

She needed this to go well. Even if the gig wasn't permanent, every penny counts.

"Excellent! Well, I won't ask you any more questions. I'll save them for the interview!" Chrissy lifted a forkful of peas. "Eat up!"

Val relaxed a little. A part of her felt like she could ace this.

As soon as Missy had scraped off everything on her plate, she spoke to Chrissy.

"Hey so like, can I leave now?" She pointed a thumb at Val. "I really don't want to be here when you interview this chick."

Chrissy sighed. "Sure, Miss. Go right ahead."

"Nice!"

She jumped up and walked fast to the doorway. It closed with a loud bang behind her.

Sissy had finished eating too. She put her fork and knife down and started bouncing up and down in her seat.

"Whoa! Chrissy, I've gotta pee!"

The blonde looked at her with a deadpan expression.

"You can go to the bathroom, Siss. It's alright."

"Woo!"

The vixen bounded for the door and disappeared from the room in about a quarter of a jizzspurt.

Only Val and her interviewer remained. Val looked down at her plate. She had been eating very slowly, savoring each bite. Nowadays, it was rare for her to eat something this good.

"Take your time, Valorie!" Chrissy stood up and grabbed her finished plate in one hand. "I'll bring the dirty dishes to the kitchen."

The interviewer circled the table to pick up the other two plates and walked to the other room. In the back of her head, Val rehearsed every answer she had prepared that morning.

Val was done eating by the time Chrissy returned. She was ready.

The boss lady sat across from her. "So, would you mind if I ask you a few questions now?"

Val breathed in, breathed out. "No ma'am. Please ask away."

"Awesome!" Chrissy flipped her chair around and sat in it backward. "Let's see here…"

The applicant got the impression that her interviewer didn't prepare much for this appointment. The blonde yawned briefly before blurting her first question.

"I got it! OK, so, what exactly are you looking for in this gig? Like, what makes you want to be one of our bartenders?"

Money was the first thing that popped into Val's mind.

"I like serving people and, uh, I like making people happy. If only just for a little bit."

Chrissy smirked. "Gotcha. So I take it you've worked in a lot of bars, right?"

"Yeah, you can say that." Val knew three was well south of 'a lot.'

"Sweet! That'll certainly make the job easier." The blonde leaned back in her chair. "Next question!"

Footsteps could be heard overhead, followed by unintelligible yelling and laughter. Dust floated down from the worn-out ceiling above.

"Girls!" Chrissy stood up on her seat and banged twice on the floorboard above. The noise disappeared. "Haha, sorry about that!" Val's empty plate now had a full serving of dust on it.

"Anyway, I wanted to ask if you'd be comfortable mixing a few drinks while you're here. You know…" Blondie winked. "Just to see how good you are with your liquor!"

Val audibly gulped. She had no choice.

"Y-Yeah, sure! Sounds like fun."

"Amazing! Let me go get the goods." Chrissy leaped off her seat and sauntered into the kitchen. A bead of sweat rolled down Val's brow. She wasn't ready after all.

The blonde strolled back into the room with three empty glasses and a tray of ice cubes in one hand and a tote bag in the other. She sat down again and placed a half dozen bottles of tequila, whiskey, amaretto and coffee liqueur on the table. A jigger, cocktail shaker and bar spoon followed.

She slid one glass close to Val and folded her hands with a grin. The prospect stared at the empty cylinder with a nervous expression.

"Alrighty! How about you start with a Brave Bull?"

One part coffee liqueur, two parts tequila. Val could see herself mixing the cocktail in her mind, but struggled to summon the courage to make it. She closed her eyes and breathed in, breathed out.

Images of her mother's smile flashed beneath her eyelids.

Val opened her eyes and grabbed the open bottles of liqueur and tequila across the table. She popped a few ice cubes into the glass, then placed the jigger in front of her and carefully poured each type of alcohol into the double cup. She put the ingredients into the cylinder, mixed them with the spoon and slid the completed cocktail over to Chrissy.

"T-There you go."

"Excellent!" The vixen lifted the glass to her lips. "Now for the good part."

She scarfed down the Brave Bull in seconds. Val looked on, simultaneously worried and amazed.

Ice cubes chinked as Chrissy placed her glass back on the table. She licked her lips and thought for a moment before speaking.

"I think you could've mixed it a little better, but not bad!" She lifted another cylinder and set it in front of Val. "Now make me a Rusty Nail."

One heavy cocktail after another. Val was focused now. She grabbed more ice cubes from the tray, sprinkled them into the glass, and reached for bottles of whiskey and liqueur. She felt like she could do this one with her eyes closed. After measuring out the ingredients and mixing them, she slid the Rusty Nail to her interviewer.

"H-Here it is."

"That was fast!" Chrissy picked up the cocktail. "I like that!"

She winked before once again downing the cocktail in seconds. Val thought this chick must be really good at drinking games.

When she was finished, the blonde sat the glass on the table and wiped her mouth with the back of her sleeve. "That was even better than the first. Well done!"

Val smiled. For the first time during this interview, she felt confident.

"Last cocktail! Make me an Orgasm."

As the boss lady put a third empty glass in front of Val, the candidate looked wide-eyed at the cylinder. She had no idea what an Orgasm was.

Chrissy noticed the girl's hesitation. "Is something wrong?"

Val had to snap out of it. She needed this.

"N-No, not at all."

She looked at the other bottles she had yet to use. Amaretto and cream liqueur were probably a part of this one. She had a feeling that another liqueur was involved.

Val put her hunch to the test. She poured a bit of amaretto and cream liqueur into the cocktail shaker and added a second liqueur she already used. When ready, she drained the shaker's contents into the glass, then slid the cocktail over to Chrissy.

"H-Here's your Orgasm."

Her interviewer lifted the glass to her lips. "You sure about this one?"

The hairs on the back of Val's neck stood up. She fucked up.

"Y-Yeah, go for it."

It was too late now.

Chrissy downed this cocktail just as effortlessly as the others. She placed the glass on the table when done and looked at Val with a blank expression.

"I think we're done here."

***

A frown hung off Val's face as she stumbled through an STD-invested subway tunnel. Apart from the flies, she was alone.

She sat down on the nearest shart-stained bench and stared into the nighttime quiet ahead.

In moments like these, Val missed her mother.

She crossed her arms and dug her head into her lap. Her train was fucking late.

The girl returned to her apartment well after midnight. She swayed across the living room with the grace of a peg-legged hooker and collapsed onto her torn-up sofa.

She fucked up. Badly.

Val respawned in the early afternoon. After yawning and scratching her crotch for about five minutes, she looked to the front door and noticed she had mail.

She walked over and picked up the blank letter envelope. It wasn't sealed. The piece of paper inside read:

'Hey Valorie!

It was nice meeting you yesterday. We'd like to chat with you a little more tonight. Can you meet us at 'Suck Bang Blow' at 11? Please bring the ring!

With love,

Chrissy'

Val looked back inside the envelope. A white ring sat in the corner.

She sat down on her sofa and sank deep into the stained stuffing. Her intuition told her she should stay home tonight.

Then her stomach grumbled.

***

Val showed up at the bar 10 minutes early, dressed in the same attire she wore the day before.

"ID please."

A gigantic security guard looked down on her. After fumbling through her wallet, she silently gave the man her ID. She couldn't believe she was still being carded.

The man let her pass. Val strolled up to the counter, sat on a stool and analyzed the crowd. The usual horndogs, whores and closet weeaboos were in full force that night.

A fuckaroo stumbled his way to the bar and slammed his glass inches away from Val's hand. In a stupid vibrato, he began chanting, "Li… quor? Li… quor? Li… quor? Li… quor? Liquor? Liquor! Liquor! Liquor! Liquor!" It sounded worse than anime dubs.

He ended his monologue with a cranial slam dunk into the counter. Ignoring the unconscious drunkard, a bartender walked up to Val.

"What are you having tonight, sweety?"

Val considered whether she should get something before Chrissy showed up. She looked at her phone. It was two minutes to 11.

"I'll get an Orgasm," Val ordered in a vain attempt to retroactively do her interview right. If she could see how it was mixed, she could see how close she was. After the look on Chrissy's face yesterday, Val figured she only got two elements right: it had liquor and it was in a glass, but even that much she was starting to doubt.

The bartender nodded and went away. Val looked at the drooling man next to her. She wondered what could've made him so unhappy.

She glanced at her phone again. Five minutes past 11. Chrissy may be running a little late. Not a big deal.

The bartender placed Val's cocktail on the counter. The candidate sipped on her drink, trying hard to suppress her nervousness. She might've drinken it a little too fast.

It was ten past 11 by the time Val finished her drink. She took the ring out of her pocket and looked at it under the dim light. It was incredibly plain.

She spun it around. The bartender asked if she would like another drink.

"Yes, please."

Val spun the ring around again and again until the bartender came back with another Orgasm. It was twenty past 11 now.

The interviewee drank her second cocktail faster than her first. She began thinking that she may have gone to the wrong bar. She finished her drink before she could tell herself to slow down.

She may have fucked up badly again. Her stomach moaned.

The bartender came back and asked her if she wanted a third round. Val nodded instinctively. She had no way of paying for all these drinks.

She looked down at the ring she was playing with. She thought she might as well wear the first piece of new jewelry she'd had in an embarrassingly long time.

Val disappeared before she could have that third cocktail.

Chapter 3
The Third Nipple

Val dreamed she laid in a flower meadow, the sun above lightly radiating her pale skin. She smelled the fresh springtime and remembered the picnics she had with her mother in the countryside.

She wished she was a kid again. Worthwhile Saturday morning television. Holographic trading cards. Commercial-free Internet videos. A home-cooked meal after homework was done.

Nowadays, life isn't so simple.

Val smelled something burning. She opened her eyes and craned her head above the tall flowers.

A fire engulfed the meadow a few meters behind her. Smoke billowed high and blanketed half the sky in darkness.

Val quickly stood up and immediately noticed her superbum attire had metamorphosed into a polka-dot dress. Though it was pretty kawaii, the alarming wall of fire was priority one on the WTF list.

Ignoring her bizarre change of outfit, Val began running toward a nearby hill, away from the flames behind her. The flowers beneath her bare feet flattened. Every step felt frighteningly real.

As smoke consumed the light blue overheard, a sadness washed over the girl. Whether she liked it or not, nothing lasts forever.

A drizzle pelted her by the time she summited the hill. She turned around and saw that the fire had extinguished itself right around where she previously laid.

She looked forward again and spotted a short little house on the prairie beneath her. A light flickered in one of its windows.

Val walked briskly to the front door and knocked. She waited a minute before trying again. It seemed like no one was home.

The gooseflesh on Val's arms told her that the temperature was dropping fast, and kawaii dresses are rarely made for the cold. She tried knocking once more. The door softly opened in response.

The candidate warily stepped inside, closing the door behind her. The space was largely empty. A fireplace burned on the opposite wall and illuminated a carpet with a pillow and folded blanket on top.

Val tiptoed to the carpet, the wooden floorboards lightly creaking beneath her feet. The carpet kissed her soles with warmth. She knelt by the fireplace and warmed her hands.

As heat flowed through Val's body, she couldn't help but wonder how bizarre her dream was. The fire, the smoke and the cabin weren't tied to any of her memories. It was like she was in another person's head.

She looked down at her dress and wondered what that was all about, too. Outside of old photographs, she had never seen anyone wear anything like it.

Val continued kneeling by the fireplace a little while longer. Despite the oddness of her situation, the bouncing flames in front of her made her feel at ease.

She closed her eyes and drifted back to the days of electric mice and spiky-haired dualists. She thought about the time her mother bought her two completely new starter decks after finals one year, and the time they ordered way too many tacos at that terrible Mexican place. They both grew to know their toilet very well after that episode.

She thought about the time they went to Sea Universe and fed a hot dog to a lobster, and when her mother clumsily bumped into a lamppost while walking her home from school. It's like she could see it happen in slow motion.

Val quickly grew tired. She opened her eyes and stood up. It was pitch dark out. She scanned every wall and corner she could, looking for signs of hidden cameras or hatches. She walked over to the front door and twisted a small switch to lock it. Though she hadn't been awake for long, her mind told her it was time to rest again.

She picked up the pillow and blanket and positioned them closer to the fireplace. She tucked herself underneath the wool and sunk her head deep into the pillow, staring at the flames that continued to dance in front of her.

Val thought more about her mother, combing through more memories she had of her. If this really was her dream, she wondered why mom wasn't there beside her.

Her eyes were heavy. She closed them and pictured her mother's face beneath her eyelids. She wished she could be as pretty as she was when she grew up.

She tried to remember what they had during their last picnic. She knew that they made PB&J sandwiches the night before and that they brought those lemon-flavored cookies with them, but she forgot what else they had on the side.

The fire in front of her dimmed. Was it strawberries, cantaloupe or mangoes? Three totally different tastes, but Val was never any good with food. She definitely remembered it was sweet.

The fireplace had extinguished completely. Val nestled beneath her blanket, trying to retain as much heat she could before it escaped into the dark, cold room around her.

Something started to smell. Badly. At first Val dismissed it as burning wood from the fireplace, but the odor started getting stronger the longer she laid there. She peeked her head outside her blanket.

A black and white linoleum floor stretched on as far as the eye could see. A shirtless, bleeding cadaver ambled toward her. And she thought the wall of fire was going to be the worst of it.

The young girl panicked. She hastily crawled away, her wide eyes fixed on the undead creature that spilled red behind itself. Splinters burrowed deep into the palms of her hand just before she slammed the back of her head against the cabin's front-facing wall.

She sprang to her feet and lunged to the front door. She twisted the lock switch and tried pulling the knob. It wouldn't open.

Val looked behind her. The cadaver was only a few feet away from the cabin now.

She tried twisting and pulling the knob harder, but the door felt as if it was glued shut. She quickly went to the window. The meadow was gone. Nothing but darkness remained.

She could hear the floorboard creak as the corpse took its first step in the home. Its putrid stench made Val want to vomit.

The novice bartender dared to turn around and stare at the drooling carcass that was about to devour her. The red-eyed, emaciated figure hunched low. Its arms violently shook each time it moved.

Val sank to the floor, tears softly streaming down her cheeks. She couldn't believe how rapidly this pleasant dream of hers had become a nightmare.

She closed her eyes and waited to wake up. She tried hard to ignore the zombie's steps, its stench and how terrifyingly real this fantasy was.

She pictured her mother's warm, loving face in her mind. She hoped that she would get to see her again in the next dream.

Suddenly, the footsteps stopped. Val waited a minute. She thought that maybe it was all over, that her nightmare had decided to show her some mercy.

She opened her eyes again. The monster scratched at a gleaming chain wrapped around its waist.

It flew back to the linoleum fast. Just as it left the cabin, someone back fisted its skull from behind. The zombie hit the floor sideways, its viscera splattering everywhere. A pointed heel buried deep into its cranium for good measure.

Val rubbed her eyes hard as a familiar bitch strode toward her.

The short-haired vixen crossed her arms and grimaced a few feet away from Val.

"What in sweet fuck are you doing?"

Val stared at Missy with her mouth wide open. Her savior looked uncharacteristically cute in a housedress similar to her own. She struggled hard to make sense of what she just witnessed.

"Yeah, you have no idea what the hell is going on. I get it." The moody girl walked up to Val, grabbed her wrist and lifted her to her feet. "But I'm not good with this kind of shit. I'll let Chrissy explain when we catch up to her."

Val's eyes grew wide. Her skin had goosebumps. "W-W-Wait."

Missy rolled her eyes and put her hands on her hips. She sighed heavily. "Yeah yeah yeah, here we go again. Let's hear it."

Val looked desperately into Missy's eyes for answers. "Isn't this just a dr-dr-dream? This isn't r-r-real." She smiled nervously. "This is just one of those tr-trippy dreams of mine, right?"

The smoker closed her eyes and shook her head. "You're really not cut out for this."

"What's going on?!" Val stepped in front of Missy, tears welling underneath her eyes. "Please…"

"I need a cigarette." Missy dug into her bra and pulled out a pack of cloves and a lighter. She ignited a wand, breathed in and squatted. She looked Val straight in the eye and spoke.

"This ain't your dream, cunt."

Val stared back intensely. She tried hard not to cry. "W-W-What?"

Missy took a moment to suck on her cigarette. She tried not to lose her patience.

"This isn't your dream, numbnuts. It's someone else's." She rolled her stick between her fingers aggressively. "We go into people's heads, kill their nightmares and get the fuck out. It's our thing."

Missy's words made no sense to Val. Her mind was in tatters, still desperately trying to make out what the hell was going on. She couldn't say much in reply.

"This is so… weird."

"Whatever dude." The abrasive bartender wiped her cigarette on the floor and stood up. "Let's get a fucking move on already."

Missy walked toward the nothingness ahead. Val stood and watched on, eyes still wide. She didn't know what to do.

The chain-wielder turned around after a few minutes. She yelled to the candidate. "If you want a job, follow me! If you don't, just fucking stand there!" She walked backward with a smirk on her face, then added. "And don't bother with a follow-up email!"

Val remembered the crackers and ramen noodles. She took her first step forward. She breathed in, breathed out and ran to Missy in the distance.

The pothead shook her head and giggled when the applicant finally caught up to her. Missy couldn't help but think Chrissy fucked up with this one.

The pair trekked ahead in silence. Val turned around constantly, half-expecting another zombie to lunge at her. Nothing but a thin horizon line beckoned them forward.

Val couldn't subdue her unease. She tried to divert attention from the millions of questions that swirled in her head. She focused on her breath and the steps that echoed in that blank vacuum. Neither seemed to work.

She had to indulge herself.

"D-D-Do you know where we're going?"

Missy gave her a dirty sideways glance. "Well sure, I'm heading toward the nearest landmark," she sarcastically said within the endless white void. "Do I look like I know where the fuck I'm going? I'm just walking until something happens."

What was that supposed to mean? Val's question just opened a can of worms. She couldn't help herself.

"W-What do you think… is going to happen?"

Missy sighed. "Can you *not* hear with your eyes, dumbass? I don't know because we're inside some fucko's head. This is *his* nightmare. We've got nothing to do with it."

"Oh, I s-see. And..." Missy's vague answers didn't help much. For her own sake, Val decided not to pry further. "...nevermind."

The short-tempered girl scoffed. The two continued forward, waiting for something to happen.

Still on edge, Val stared at the hem of her dress to distract herself. She admired how it bounced with every step. She wished she could be just as whimsical and carefree, at least for a moment.

The white ring on Val's hand glimmered as they pressed on. She looked at Missy's hand and noticed she wore a similar accessory, only blue. If this was real, she wondered if the jewelry had anything to do with it.

Their footsteps reverberated throughout the white space. Val tried hard to focus on her breathing and remove herself from her anxiety. The apprehension was taking over.

Missy's steps creaked. She held a hand up to Val, ordering her to stop in her tracks. She then kneeled, placed an ear to the floor and listened.

After a few seconds, she got back up, dug into her bra and pulled out a slender steel flask. She undid the cap, guzzled down her portable Rusty Nail and grinned.

"This is it, chicken shit."

Missy concealed her flask and materialized chains with a wave of her hand. She poked at the floor with her heel to find the right spot to pummel. Val stared wide-eyed, her body desperately telling her to run in the opposite direction.

"You ready, little dick?"

Val continued to stand motionless, her mind struggling to find the right words to say.

"I… don't—"

"That's a yes then!" Missy raised her heel high. "Giddy-up, motherfucker."

She slammed her foot down hard into the linoleum. It cracked far in every direction, then swallowed the girls whole.

Val quickly fell inside. She could barely see a thing beneath her. The darkness rushed past.

Tears sped off her eyes into the abyss behind her. She thought she was going to die.

She tried to imagine her mother in front of her. She desperately sketched every line of her kind face in her head.

Before she could finish her portrait, Val crashed face-first into a flat, hard surface. Her body writhed in pain, and she instinctively curled up in a ball on the floor. She coughed, struggling to regain an ounce of breath.

Having landed safely on two feet, Missy looked on in disgust. "We fell, like, six feet dude."

Val rolled over in agony, her face still wincing from her woefully miscalculated fall. It felt like her nose was buried in her skull. She wanted to wake up now.

Missy shook her head. She whispered, "I don't get paid enough for this shit."

Val opened her eyes and pushed herself to a sitting position. Rocks jutted out from the walls of the hidden room they discovered. The floor beneath her was similar to the one she just fell through, only covered in a thick layer of grime. She turned her head to Missy and noticed a beat-up wooden door behind her partner.

"W-What's that?"

"Seriously? What the hell does it look like?"

The prospect thought she saw a shadow move under the doorframe. Her anxiety quickly set in once more.

"We're not going to open it, are we?"

"No. We're going to climb out of here, grab some ice cream and fuck each other until the sun comes up." Missy walked over, grabbed Val's shoulder and lifted her to a standing position. She looked Val in the eyes before she spoke again. "Grow some balls, kiddo."

Val froze in terror, her heart beating fast again. She looked down at the white ring on her finger. She decided it was time to escape.

Just as Missy grabbed the door's knob, Val pulled the jewelry on her hand. It wouldn't budge.

She looked at it closely, then tried twisting it. After, she rubbed the sweat in her hands together. Nothing worked.

The smoker stared at Val disapprovingly. She watched Val attempt to remove her ring a few more times before interjecting.

"It won't come off unless someone takes it off for you." She grinned. "And I'm sure as shit not doing that."

Val desperately pulled on the ring one last time. Nothing. Without an alternative, she jumped to Missy and pleaded.

"P-P-Please! I'm not ready for what's behind t-this door." Tears welled in her eyes. "Let's find another way…"

"Too late!" Missy grabbed Val by the shoulder and, in one swift motion, flung her back to the opposite side of the room. Val skidded on her ass in shock.

Missy crossed her arms and grimaced. "Listen, Vagina. Whether you like it or not, we're knee-deep in some sicko's head. The only way out of here is to open this door, kill whatever monsters we find and save this dude before he kills himself. That's the name of the game."

Val searched Missy's face for mercy. She found none. "B-B-But... I'm not ready."

Her partner sighed loudly. "How many of your ex-boyfriends have you whimpered *that* to? Just shut the fuck up already."

With a dangerous kick, Missy blew the door straight off its hinges. It crashed immediately into a line of zombies on the other side. The foul-mouthed assassin smugly charged forward and quickly leveled up her melee ability with the mutilated family jewels of her opponents.

Val crawled back across the brown linoleum in a panic, bumping her head against the pointed rocks on the opposite wall. She looked up at the hole that Missy created. It was time for plan B.

The candidate shot up and found a pair of low rocks to dig her feet into. She reached out and grabbed onto two protrusions above, then summoned what little upper body strength she had to hoist herself slightly higher on the wall.

As Missy continued to bathe in warm glory, a visitor slowly hobbled into the hidden room. Val didn't notice.

Lines of salvia oozed out of the red-eyed monster's jaws. It scratched at its dried skin constantly, opening patches of red along its face and appendages. Its stench was intolerable.

As Val searched for more footing, a whiff of the creature's odor floated into her nostrils. Her mind went blank in fear.

Maybe if she didn't look back, everything would just disappear.

The fiend lunged for Val's legs. Just before its fingernails dug into her, something crashed into its spine hard.

The zombie's fragile parts splashed all over the room. A familiar blonde stood on top of its torso, her legs covered entirely in red. She wore a housedress similar to Val's, only noticeably stained with the blood of her previous conquests.

Chrissy stepped out of the blown-up cadaver and kicked it to the side of the room, right next to an arm. She turned and smiled at Val.

"Hey there Valorie! Glad to see you're alive and everything. Welcome to the physical part of your interview!"

Still clinging onto the wall, Val glanced backward. Fresh gore dripped from the boundaries around her savior. Her attacker's body lay naked, face-up in the light. It had a third nipple.

So this wasn't a dream, after all.

Val dropped from the wall, unconscious.

Chrissy caught her head in one hand before it slammed on the ground. She chuckled. "Aww. Poor thing."

She picked up Val's body and slung it across her left shoulder. She could hear Missy chopping away in the room behind them.

"Let's see what Miss is up to, OK?"

The smoker just finished driving a medieval ax through a zombie's skull as her leader entered through the shattered doorway. This place looked identical to the never-ending plane they had come from, complete with a thin horizon line in the distance.

Chrissy yelled ahead to her associate, just as the stoner finished spitting onto an enemy on the white linoleum floor.

"Missy! Why the hell did you leave Val all alone back there?!"

The short-haired girl wiped some blood off her face, looked at Chrissy's cargo and remembered. "Oh shit. That's right."

She dropped her ax and walked over to meet her employer halfway.

"Is she alive and everything?"

Chrissy sighed and gently placed Val on the ground. "Yeah, she's alive. But if I didn't show up when I did, she'd probably be dead."

The blonde crossed her arms and looked into Missy's eyes. Her bartender glanced away, scratching her head.

"Shit. Sorry about that."

"Missy." Chrissy grabbed her employee's shoulders. "I know being a babysitter isn't what you signed up for, but we've all got to be responsible here." She looked down. "This can't turn out like last time."

Missy nodded. "Yeah, I know." She turned away and walked a few feet back. "I'll be better."

Chrissy grinned. "Thanks, Miss."

The dopehead looked for cigarettes inside her dress. "Yeah, you got it."

"Alrighty then!" Chrissy turned and looked at their sleeping Val. "We've got our work cut out for us!"

"I'd say." Missy squatted and ignited a wand. Smoking had always been a good friend to her. That and Chrissy, of course.

Just after her second pull, she squinted and noticed something far away.

"Chris… do you see something over there?"

Missy pointed to a moving spot in the distance. Chrissy narrowed her eyes intensely. After a few seconds, she scratched her head and sighed.

"It's a whole horde." She looked back at Val. "Looks like we're gonna have to fall back."

An explosion boomed from the faraway place. A tiny dot soared in the air.

Missy dropped her cigarette and crushed it under her heel. "Fucking Sissy."

Another blast resounded just as Val cracked her eyes open. Chrissy noticed and hopped toward her.

"Valorie!" She flashed a bright smile and kneeled over the half-awake candidate. "Welcome to the not-so-real world!"

At first disoriented, Val's fear set in as soon as she noticed she had not awakened in a good place. Looking at Chrissy's cheery face above, all she could do was force a smile.

"H-Hey there, ma'am." She rotated her head and noticed a blob moving in the distance. "H-How are you?"

"Never been better! Well, apart from the fact I've got something squishy in her shoes." She readjusted her heel behind her back. "More importantly, how are you?"

Still half grinning, Val stared into Chrissy's bright blue eyes. For some reason, she forgot her anxiety when she looked there. "I'm… alright."

"Great!" The blonde stood up excitedly. "So, here's what we're going to do!" She motioned Missy to come over. The smoker rolled her eyes, crossed her arms and dragged her feet toward the duo.

"Miss, you and I are going to head over there and help out Sissy. Valorie…" The prospect continued laying on the floor. "Please stay here and keep a good eye on your surroundings. If anything—and I mean *anything*—approaches you, run as fast as you can toward us. Got it?"

Images of an exploding zombie flashed in Val's mind. Her eyes opened wide. "Got it."

"Alrighty!" Chris dug into her bra and produced a metal tin. She unscrewed the cap, took a sip and fluffed up her hair. "You ready, Miss?"

The short-haired girl yawned and cracked her back. "Ready."

Chrissy returned her alcohol and crouched low on the ground in a sprinting position. "On your marks."

Miss sunk into a similar stance. "Get set!"

Val pushed herself up and noticed the two grinning at each other.

"Go!"

They rocketed forward in a flurry. The surge of wind blew back Val's messy hair and temporarily blinded her.

A loud bang reverberated through the void shortly thereafter. Val stared ahead, still somewhat disbelieving her current situation. Then she turned around and noticed dozens of bodies behind her.

Chrissy and Missy sped through the horde like a bullet, the former detonating zombies with her fists and the latter slicing them with her blades. The pair stopped in the middle. Miss waved chains into her hands and carved a sizable circumference around them, her steel shattering every deformed head it came into contact with.

Chris yelled above the moans. "Where's Siss?"

Miss wrapped her chains around her forearms and yelled back. "No fucking clue!"

A rocket flew over their heads and spiraled downward. It facialed a moving carcass clenching its jaw a few meters away from the pair, sending it and six other lucky contestants on an all-expense-paid trip to hell.

As the clouds from the explosion dissipated, Chris noticed that the gap it made was already filled with zombies who didn't give two shits about stepping on a duodenum.

In the opposite direction, another blast sent a mutilated troop flying. Dressed in a bright floral dress, Sissy somersaulted out from the crowd and landed on her feet next to a disgusted Missy.

"Hey bitch."

She hugged her colleague and kissed her on the cheek. "Miss me?"

Missy pushed her away and spat on the floor. "Don't fucking touch me."

"Siss!" Chrissy continued scanning the perimeter of approaching zombies. "Nice of you to join us!"

The pigtailed redhead threw up a peace sign. Chris glanced and smiled.

"You two have any idea how we're gonna get out of this?"

Sissy sprouted two MP5s in her hands and rested them on her shoulders. "All I know is that I'm going to make even more explosions! Yay!"

Missy scoffed. "Sissy must know some secret about these bums. She's probably ridden all their dicks by now."

The redhead giggled in reply. "Missy, the only dick I'll ever ride is yours."

"I will choke you."

"Kinky!"

"Girls!" Chrissy facepalmed. "Are you being serious right now? We've got a job to do here. That's not to mention the fact that we're still conducting an interview. I need you girls to stop arguing and cooperate, got it?"

The two employees hung their heads in penance.

"My bad homie."

"Right. Sorry."

Chrissy cleared her throat. She noticed the zombies were still at a safe distance. "Let's go over things. From what I gather, there's no beginning or end to this place. There may be odd holes here and there, but they don't lead anywhere."

Sissy nodded at every other word while Missy squinted sideways at her.

"This place spits out hordes like this randomly. The guy we're looking for is most likely in one of these hordes, so let's keep an eye on anything unusual. The instant you find our target, capture it. We'll regroup and return to Val. I'll start teaching her the ins and outs of the business from there. Everyone clear?"

Siss continued nodding strangely while Miss poked at something in her teeth.

"Yessir!"

"Yeah, got it."

Chrissy took out her tin and examined its contents. "I've got about a fourth left. You guys?"

Her employees inspected their flasks.

"Samesies!"

"Eh, I've got about half left."

"Good." Chrissy took a 360 degree look around them. The zombies were closing in.

"In that case, Missy, please use your chains to clear out a crapload of these guys once me and Sissy jet out of here. Siss, use your guns to help Miss. I'll fly to the opposite side and start wiping out these suckers from there."

Chrissy clenched her fists. "Everybody good?"

Missy unwrapped her chains and smirked. "Let's get this party started already."

Her leader chuckled. "I like your attitude! Siss, I'll go first." She crouched low. "See you two later!"

Chrissy bounced high into the air and disappeared behind them. Sissy sunk into a similar position and winked at Missy. "Love you, honey bun."

Missy gave her the finger. Smiling, Siss jolted up, her submachines spread out in front of her.

"Yippee-ki-yay, motherfuckers!"

Bullets streaked across corpora callosa as chains ripped through one prostate gland after another. Up an ass and around the corner, a pair of balls dropped for one crusty corpse as it ran toward a voluminous blonde. Chrissy pulled some kung pao shit and, with the palm of her hand, sent the numbnuts flying backward, crashing and disassembling his sausage party. More voyeurs filled the space. Chrissy smiled.

Eyeballs bulged and popped under pressure. Limbs and other funny things flew like vultures in the blood mist. Even at a distance, Val could hear steel tearing up squishy insides. It was almost hypnotizing.

Val sat on the white floor with a confused expression, still searching for a logical explanation to this madness. She was too lost in thought to notice a small dark spot appear on the ground adjacent to her, expanding and contracting quietly as if it were breathing.

The ball grew larger with every exhale. Val finally detected it from the corner of her eye when it had swelled into the size of a basketball.

"What the hell?!"

Frightened, she crawled backward on all fours. From what she determined to be a safe distance, she watched the orb grow larger with each of its breaths.

Val approached the circle cautiously when it became a little bigger than an exercise ball. Little by little, she crawled to the edge and poked the black dot with a finger.

As soon as her index touched the ground, a deafening shriek echoed inside her head.

SCREEEEECH

Val pulled away immediately, her heart racing fast. She glanced at the faraway horde, then looked back down at the expanding circle. It breathed out again, growing into a small spotlight.

Something bad was coming, and Val didn't want to be there when it arrived.

She sprang up and ran toward the other girls. She stopped a dozen meters away from the horde.

Val could hear bones snap above the zombie moans. Her legs trembling, she clasped her hands together and tried to find a sliver of courage inside her.

"C-C…"

This interview was *a lot* harder than she thought it'd be.

"Chrissy!"

A wall of drooling, emaciated monsters looked back. Val nearly pissed herself. One lunged forward without hesitation.

Blondie dropped from the sky and swung her hand out in front of her. The zombie ran its head right into it. She grabbed the beast's skull and pushed down, squishing it into its torso until it formed a goop of bubbling nonsense.

The zombie's companions sought revenge. Chrissy waited for all of them to come in close, then ran a fist through each of their faces in one swift motion.

She jumped back and landed right beside Val. "Hey girl! What's up?" Red oozed off her hands.

Val was shivering. "I-I…" She looked down at the ocean waves of blood running beneath her feet. After shaking her head, she turned to Chrissy and looked her in the eyes.

"I f-found something. Something strange."

Chris' face brightened. "You don't say! Where is it?"

"It's…" Val rotated and pointed behind her. Then she saw the circle moving toward them.

"It's almost here."

Chrissy hopped in place excitedly. "Way to go Valorie! This is amazing!" She turned and called for her employees to join. "Girls!"

An explosion rumbled from the opposite end of the crowd. Sissy soared into the air, scattering a handful of cooked grenades and igniting more zombies before settling by her leader. Four clouds of fire erupted into the air as she put up a peace sign and made an ahegao face.

Missy sliced through the horde with a shield and a halberd. By the time she made it to the other side, she boasted a collection of gleaming heads in her weapon's shaft.

One by one, the zombies turned to face their targets. Chrissy noticed.

"Fall back!"

Chrissy grabbed Val by the armpit and sped away from the mob. Sissy and Missy followed close behind.

In midair, she spotted what Val was talking about.

"Is that black dot what you saw?"

Wind roaring in her ears, Val tried yelling back. "Yeah! And it's growing!"

Chrissy skidded to a stop. Val attempted to do the same, but fell flat on her face around her interviewer's feet. She rose quickly, blushing slightly.

Sissy and Missy ground up beside them. They all stared at the festering circle in front of them. It was the size of a pond now.

The blonde placed her hands on her shoulders. She walked up to the edge of the vortex as it continued breathing and expanding. The other girls watched. Val could feel her stomach stirring.

"I think we've found our guy, ladies." Chrissy smiled. "You can thank Valorie for that. Well done!"

Sissy clapped unenthusiastically while Missy picked her nose.

"Congrats yo."

"Meh."

"Now we've got to figure out how exactly we're going to get rid of this thing. Anyone have any ideas?"

Missy flicked a booger. "Nope."

"Val?" Chrissy beamed another grin at her. "What do you think?"

The prospect crossed her arms and scratched at her elbow nervously. "I… don't—"

"What about explosions?!" Sissy whipped out a bazooka. "Those always seem to work!"

"I think this is a bit different, Siss." Chrissy crouched down by the circle. She watched it grow another few inches. "I don't think we'll be able to blast our way out of this one."

SCREEEEECH

A piercing shriek emanated from the blot. The girls winced and covered their ears. When the scream was over, Val opened her eyes and saw scores of zombies standing in the circle.

Chrissy moved ahead of her. "Girls, drink up!" She dug into her dress, took out her flask and offered it to Val. "Have the rest of this. You might need it."

Val grabbed the tin, unscrewed the cap and took a whiff of the alcohol. She looked at Chrissy incredulously.

"W-What?"

"Just drink it." Fisticuffs tossed her hair. "I'll tell you more later."

Val looked into the bottle and examined the dark liquid within. She shook her head in disbelief.

"Valorie." Chrissy turned and stared Val in the eyes. She had her attention. "Please."

The candidate did what she was told. She gulped down the booze, thinking it tasted something like a Brave Bull. She handed the empty tin back to Chrissy.

"Thank you." The blonde returned the flask to its happy place. The monsters swayed their way toward them. "Now get the hell outta here."

She didn't have to say that twice. Val about-faced and sprinted past Sissy and Missy, the former of which kneeled and aimed her bazooka at a trio of douches a few yards away. A rocket-propelled grenade detonated in the jaw of a hapless cadaver seconds after.

Val ran until her lungs were exhausted. She bent over and caught her breath as sounds of mutilation echoed behind her. Mentally, physically and emotionally, she was drained.

Something nearby caused the ground to vibrate. At first Val assumed it to be the calamity behind her, but the tremors grew more powerful.

She opened her eyes, staring at the blank floor beneath her. Sweat dripped from her forehead and collected into tiny transparent pools below. The sound of one hundred steps approaching made her clutch her head in anxiety.

She looked up. Another horde danced a short distance away. It formed a wall blocking her only means of escape.

Val collapsed to the ground. She was too exhausted to be brave. She just wanted to wake up.

The homely girl kneeled in her sweat, ready for this nightmare to be over. She figured that even if she did die, she might get to have breakfast with mom again.

The zombies swarmed around Val when they arrived, careful not to dig in headfirst lest they be pummeled in one swoop. Val continued to kneel, even as her heart pulsed faster than ever before.

One of the creatures limped forward. Val stared at its hairy, blackened feet. She wouldn't dare look it in the eye.

Val waited for the beast to pounce, to sink its teeth into her skin. She continued to stare wide-eyed, hoping this will all be over fast.

The feet stopped. The beast mumbled. Something roped around Val and sunk into her waist.

She looked up. The zombie in front of her had two silver balls in its mouth. She caught a red blur behind the crowd.

Val was yanked back just before the grenades detonated. She flew through the air, failing to determine exactly what had just happened. Her ass slid on the linoleum a safe distance away from the horde.

When her body came to a full stop, the chains around her waist loosened and returned to Missy's forearm. Chrissy stood smiling beside her in the middle of a hemoglobin dust cloud.

"Another close one!" The leader walked up to Val and offered a hand. "We've got to keep a better eye on you!"

Missy whispered "what a pain in the ass" while kicking a half-conscious zombie with an exposed spinal cord.

Chrissy continued. "We took care of the dicks here, so you don't have to run anymore. We still haven't figured out our problem though." She pointed at the growing black hole. Another bang erupted in the distance. "Or that one."

As Missy carved her name into a corpse, she asked, "What the hell was up with that scream? It sounded like someone was getting fisted."

Chrissy shook her head. "No idea, but it can't be great."

More blasts resounded. Chrissy stretched.

"Miss, let's go take care of those other assholes while we come up with something." She turned to Val. "Valorie, please stay here and watch this thing. If anything weird happens, just call out my name."

Val stood there motionlessly, her dress saturated red and brown. She could hardly stand, much less alert the others of danger again.

She nodded.

"Alright! Let's get a move on, Miss."

Missy swang a second saber into her hands. "Way ahead of you."

SCREEEEECH

That sound was so head-splitting, maddening, chaotic.

SCREEEEECH

As Val clamped down hard on her ears, she witnessed a shadowy claw rise from the deathly chasm. Its giant fingers separated and cracked in the sky above them.

It slammed down hard on the girls below.

Chapter 4
Wimpy Hut Jr.

The claw slowly scraped the linoleum it splintered. Rivulets of blood flowed beneath it.

Val stared motionless at the whiteness above, her ears still ringing from the insanity.

Missy's heels clacked on the floor as she strode up to the job seeker. "That's three times now." She wrapped her chains around her forearms. "That won't happen again."

Chrissy followed close behind and offered Val a hand. "You've still got to learn one of our most important rules." The homely girl promptly latched on. "Prepare for the worst, but hope for the best!"

Val rose to her feet, her ears still deafened by their latest encounter. She could faintly hear Sissy's bombs detonate a few dozen yards away. She responded as best she could.

"R-Right. I've got to be more careful."

"It's your first time!" Chrissy stuck her thumb and grinned. "I think you're doing great so far."

Missy pretended to regurgitate.

"So..." The blonde turned to face the giant pool nearby just as the hand's fingers disappeared into the abyss. "This turned out to be a lot more complicated than I expected.

The stoner took a sip from her flask. "I'd say. How are you on alcohol?"

"All out!" Chrissy smirked. "I gave the rest of mine to Valorie."

Missy squinted disapprovingly and crossed her arms. "Uh, Chris. Not exactly the best move you could make right now."

"I'll be fine." The leader waved away her employee's concern. "Val needs it more than I do in this situation."

The short-haired girl was unconvinced. "Didn't you just say, 'Prepare for the worst, but hope for the best'? I don't know about you, but giving your alcohol to Wimpy Hut Jr. over here isn't exactly preparing for the worst-case scenario."

Chrissy shook her head. "Miss, I appreciate your concern. I really do. But the fact of the matter is that we've *all* got to make it out of here in one piece." She smiled at Val. "It's not just about us anymore."

Missy scratched her head. "Alright, you're the boss. Just don't do anything crazy."

Blondie giggled while readjusting her hair. "No promises!"

The giant pool, now the size of a football field, started to bubble and fizz. A thin layer of haze oozed out from it, as if a chemical reaction had taken place beneath the surface.

Chrissy and Missy studied the specimen as the hand from before slithered its fingers out from the left edge of the hole. Still slightly disoriented, Val watched on with eyes wide open.

"Girls..." Chrissy spread her legs and clenched her fists. "Get ready."

A second hand squirmed out from the opposite side of the chasm. Missy swung two scimitars into her hands.

The darkened fingers dug deep into the floor, hoisting whatever rose inside the void. Val looked behind her. Dozens of stray zombies averted Sissy's destruction. They were only a few yards away.

SCREEEEECH

Val panicked. She ran to Chrissy and Missy, who were both completely focused on the threat ahead of them. As the slow-moving cadavers moved in, Val noticed something in their faces.

They were crying.

SCREEEEECH

Val turned away from the horde momentarily to witness a large mass of thick, slimy tendrils rise from the dead star. Face obscured, the head rose until a gargantuan, forlorn housewife revealed herself. She wore a dress similar to the trio below.

Chrissy spun around and grabbed Val by her armpit. She kicked off into the air just as the hellish subconscious slammed down hard on the linoleum with her foot. Missy watched the pair escape as she dealt with the fiends closing in around her.

Val had trouble breathing when she landed with Chrissy a good distance away. She bent over and searched for air while the blonde quickly went to work dispatching the random zombies around them.

Neither had the chance to take it easy for long.

SCREEEEECH

The dark colossus leaped in pursuit, aiming her foot directly at Val as she came down. Chrissy rushed away from her last kill and seized the foot by its big toe, seconds before Val could be pasted.

"Val!" The leader's arms trembled. She screamed with clenched teeth. "Pay attention!"

The candidate watched on, her legs and arms trembling.

"Ragh!"

Chrissy summoned as much strength she could into her biceps. Somehow, her power matched the menacing goliath above her. She may have been even stronger.

The blonde's arms started to extend. With another yell, she pushed the monstrosity's foot back, causing it to lose balance. The distressed housewife collapsed on her flat ass, each bony cheek sending fissure lines into every direction.

Chrissy fell to her knees, panting from exhaustion. She couldn't go much further without alcohol.

"Chrissy!" Val speed to her savior. "Chrissy, are you alright?!"

Blondie stuck a thumb up. Her eyes were half-open. "Never better."

She coughed. Val looked forward and saw the leviathan already begin to stand. She slung Chrissy's arm around her neck and stood her up.

"We've got to get the hell out of here."

The pair hobbled in the opposite direction. Val saw that Sissy had almost finished wiping out the other horde. They'd have backup soon.

Val craned her neck backward. The tormented giant rose, its liquid black gaze fixed upon her. It rose until it once again resembled an inescapable black cloud overhead. The monster parted its lips and spoke.

"I hate you!"

The pair dragged its feet. Sweat dripped off Val's face as she heard the giant take its first step forward.

"Valorie..." Chrissy spoke barely above a whisper. "Great job today. I mean it."

Val struggled to form a smile. "O-Of course. But w-we're not out of here yet."

Chrissy continued. "I hope you learned a little bit about yourself today."

Val readjusted her interviewer's arm around her neck. The behemoth took another step toward them.

"And I hoped you learned… how to be brave."

The prospect could see the horde's remains more clearly now. They were almost by Sissy. Another step resounded behind them.

"Valorie… put me down."

"What?!" Val yelled. "Chrissy, we've got to keep going!"

"No." Chrissy lifted a finger and pointed to something in the distance. "Look there."

Val squinted her eyes and noticed a black circle appear by the bodies the redhead had mutilated. Her heart sank. They both stopped walking.

Val peered at the monster behind them. It was closing the distance fast.

She dropped to the floor. Chrissy patted her on the head.

"Now is not the time for this, honey." The blonde grinned weakly. "The party's just getting started. Keep looking."

Cavalcades of human-sized knives floated from the hole into the air. They readjusted themselves horizontally, aiming straight for the pair staring at them.

They accelerated forward, faster than bullets. Val cowered and screamed. Chrissy stood in place.

All the knives flew straight past them. All but one.

Blondie gripped a knife by its oversized handle in her right hand. It wiggled in an attempt to catch up to its brethren, but eventually surrendered and stopped levitating.

"This is for you." Chrissy offered the knife to Val. The prospect shook uncontrollably on the floor. "The final part... of your interview."

The housewife took one step closer. Val stared at the ridiculous weapon. "Are you s-serious?"

Chrissy smiled. "Best part of the business."

A hundred emotions stirred inside Val. She was exhausted from the stress, angry because she felt tricked, sad because the person most important to her was gone and she had nothing else to turn to.

But, above all else, she was tired of this shit.

Val eased her fingers around the knife. It was much lighter than it looked. She glimpsed at the monster and told herself it was time to fucking end this.

"Go get her, Val." Chrissy nodded. "You're ready."

Val wiped away the sweat from her face. She looked to the floor, breathed in, breathed out and ran forward.

Her heart raced as Chrissy grinned from ear to ear. The knife bounced on the linoleum, sparks flying behind it.

Tears streamed off Val's face as her feet stomped hard on the ground. The closer she got, the faster she ran.

The monster raised a foot, hoping to squish Val when she got close enough. The candidate anticipated this.

Val spun the knife in front of her and switched hands, then sped away from the goliath's first foot. She jumped, narrowly avoiding the attack, and jolted ahead toward the monster's second ankle.

She closed her eyes. She told her mother she was sorry.

Val swung the knife with all of her strength, cutting the beast's bone. Black sludge spewed out, soaking Val's dress as she ran to the opposite side and sliced again.

SCREEEEECH

The housewife bent down and reached for her bleeding ankle. Val dropped the knife and ran, afraid that she'd be caught in the giant's grasp.

Someone sprinted toward her, then flew into the air.

The colossus saw Missy approach and yelled.

"I hate you—"

Her last words were cut off by an oversized knife to the throat. The infinite whiteness of that world quickly faded to black.

***

Val stared at her third Orgasm. The drunkard from before was nowhere to be found.

A familiar blonde pulled out the stool next to her and sat down.

"Drinks on me tonight, Valorie." She smiled. "Well done."

Val glanced at Chrissy, then turned her head to the ring on the counter. "Thank you."

"So…" Blondie folded her hands. "I meant to mention this before, but as you've probably noticed, we're not actually bartenders." She giggled. "You handled things a lot better than I anticipated. A *hell* of a lot better."

Chrissy shifted in her seat. Val took a sip of her drink, trying to suppress her emerging hunger.

"The gist of the job is that we knock sense into people who've had a little too much to drink. We do that before they hurt other people or, well, hurt themselves. It's like therapy, but sexier and more badass."

Val seemed lost in thought. She continued looking down at the ring in front of her. Her stomach whimpered softly.

Chrissy went on. "We, uh, use the rings to get into people's heads. It usually requires us to get a little tipsy beforehand… that's definitely one of the fun parts. When we're on the other side, most of our bodily functions are suspended—no thirst, hunger, etc. We're always way more powerful there, for some reason, and each of us has skills based on things we like. Missy's into medieval weaponry, Sissy likes explosions, etc." She looked at Val. "Do you follow, so far?"

Val nodded her head and sipped again.

"Great! So, uh, another thing is that a second here is, like, an hour in those places. And these places are kind of based on memories or traumatizing shit people have been through in their lives. If you think about it, it's kind of what most nightmares are like."

Chrissy fluffed her hair and looked at Val again. The candidate's eyes looked tired.

"I think that's about all I have to cover." The employer pulled back her stool and stood up.

"Valorie, I would be honored if you'd agree to join our team!"

Chrissy extended her hand. Val looked her way, then turned back and took another sip of her cocktail.

"Well, what do you say?"

Val grabbed the ring off the counter before seizing Chrissy's hand.

"Thanks for the drinks."

The prospect made her way out the door. Chrissy looked at the white ring in her hand and sat back down on her stool.

Blondie smirked. "She'll be back."

Chapter 5
Party Time

Val had new mail when she woke up the next morning. This time, her landlord.

The letter pointed out she hadn't paid rent in months. The building's owner couldn't afford to keep her anymore.

She was getting evicted.

Val returned to her torn-up sofa and stared at her ceiling for a long time. After a breath, she looked down at her phone and saw the time. 11:18 AM. She was supposed to be out by noon.

She dragged her feet to the bathroom and gathered her toothbrush, toothpaste, a comb and other toiletries behind the medicine cabinet. When she was done, Val asked how she could be so incompetent.

She thought about the psychotic girls from last night and wondered how deranged she'd have to become to make a decent living in this world.

Val walked over to her closet and fit as much clothing she could into her only suitcase. She stuffed a picture of her mother into the bag before zipping up.

She headed for the front door with her belongings five minutes before noon. She couldn't hold back her tears as she twisted the handle one last time.

***

Thirty minutes later, Val looked up at the menu of her local fast-food chain with red eyes. She jingled the change in her pocket and knew she barely had enough for a soda. She sat down in a booth and dug her head into her arms, ignoring her stomach's constant moaning.

She racked her brain for places to eat. Food was the only thing she could think about. The only place she had left to try was the soup kitchen around the corner. She grabbed her luggage and exited the burger joint.

The warm summer air was disappearing fast. Val reached into her suitcase and took out her jean jacket. A gift from her mother. She smiled softly as she put it on.

There was a queue in the soup kitchen's alleyway by the time Val got there. While she waited, she cursed herself for sinking so low.

Her stomach whimpered louder than before. The smell of vegetable soup around her was overwhelming.

Val waited an hour. She desperately tried to suppress her hunger by fidgeting in place. Her senses took over when she was at the front of the line.

Her hand trembled when a volunteer offered a cup. She tried to hide her face. The saliva in her mouth nearly poured out her lips.

Val ran out of the kitchen with her portion and consumed her soup at a deserted corner in the alleyway. When she was done, she mulled over why she hated herself so much.

She couldn't find an answer before night arrived.

She cried alone in the darkness when no one was around. She lost a part of herself, something that only the best of friends could bring out in each other.

"I'm so sorry mom." Val coughed up tears of asphyxiation. "I'm… so sorry."

"There there, girly." A slim woman with a posh accent spoke a few yards away. She was obscured in shadow. "Things will only get better from here."

Val wiped her eyes, grabbed her suitcase and stood up in a hurry. She watched as the stranger stepped out from her hiding place.

The girl wore long black bangs over her right eye. Her jeans had tears in strange places and her hoodie had some Norwegian death metal band on the front. She smiled.

"How about I treat you to drinks tonight?"

Val took a few steps back. "No thank you." She'd more than learned her lesson about strange women offering her liquor.

The headbanger continued. "There's this place not too far from here. 'He Ain't Here,' I believe it's called? Meet me there if you change your mind." She about-faced. "I hope we get to know each other well soon."

She walked away, leaving Val alone again in her discomfort. As time passed, Val asked herself if things could get worse from here.

The homeless girl took a few steps further, then stopped. For a moment, she wondered if she was getting into a mess similar to yesterday's. Then she thought about how good last night's cocktail tasted.

As soon as Val spun around the corner to the alleyway, she spotted her visitor leaning on the front entrance to the soup kitchen, listening to music. She couldn't back out now.

The strange girl pulled the buds out of her ears excitedly. "Ah, you've had a change of heart! Very good, darling." She started walking down the cobblestone street, then looked back. "Let's get a move on, then."

Val followed, her head facing the ground. She told herself she'd only have one drink. Afterward, she'd somehow find a place to sleep.

"Say, mind if a friend of mine tags along?"

The former prospect lifted her face slightly. She was getting nervous. "Y-Yeah, sure."

"Excellent." The heavy metal lover walked on. After a few seconds of silence, she continued. "My name's Monica, by the way." She faced Val and smiled. "Yours?"

The homeless girl grinned weakly and replied, "I'm Valorie. You can call me Val, too."

"Ah." Monica nodded. "Fine name. You must be very noble, Valorie."

Val looked back down to the ground. "Y-Yeah… I try."

They strolled some more in the middle of the street.

"So where are you from, Miss Valorie?"

"From around here." Val was starting to feel more and more uneasy. It made sense for strangers to want to get to know each other better, but something about this stranger felt off. "What about you?"

"Abroad." Monica giggled softly. "Can't you tell?"

Val faked another smile. The girl dressed in black went on.

"Came here for work, but things didn't turn out well." She dug into her pocket. "However, one thing led to another, and now I'm pretty alright."

She turned the block with Val in tow. They continued in silence for a little more. Val stopped when their bar was in sight.

"I-I'm sorry." Val dug her hand into her jean jacket. "This was a mistake."

"Nonsense." Monica walked over and stood right in front of her. "Valorie, please look at me."

Val lifted her head and looked Monica in the eyes. Bright blue, just like the girl from yesterday.

"You've got to learn to grow some balls, love." She smirked. "It's just a drink, then we'll all be on our way."

The rocker wrapped an arm around Val. They continued to their destination.

"You know, someone close to me once said that things won't get better unless you take action." She gripped Val's shoulder. "You've got to squash those demons before they drive you insane."

Monica let go once they finally arrived. She jumped forward to the door and pushed it open. "After you, love."

Val nodded faintly and walked over. As she passed through the door frame, the rocker whispered, "For the record, if I wanted to hurt you, I would've done so by now."

Those words sent shivers down Val's spine. In that moment she knew she had definitely made a mistake.

She was past the point of no return. She breathed in, breathed out and looked over the bar.

Thankfully, it was decently crowded. Multicolored lights hung above the counter and out-of-season holiday ornaments merrily swung above the heads of patrons. A blonde with hair drills sat on a stool and smiled her way.

"Eliza!"

Monica stepped out behind Val and walked over to the counter. The pair hugged, then the headbanger motioned Val to come over.

"Miss Valorie, I'd like you to meet my longtime partner and confidant, Eliza. Eliza, meet Valorie. Val, for short."

Val offered a hand to the girl. Like her colleague, something seemed off about her. For one thing, she looked incredibly young. Too young to be in a bar, at least. Val noted the lack of a bouncer.

"Nice to meet you, Eliza."

"Same!"

The girl grabbed Val's hand and shook it. She tilted her head like a puppy and asked, "Hey, you've been crying."

Val's face reddened. Monica intervened. "Now Liza, let's not pry so early." She pulled out a stool and sat down. "My friend here can be a tad headstrong sometimes."

The out-of-work bartender pulled out a stool of her own and sat beside her. "I-It's OK."

"Anyway," Monica clapped her hands together. "How about we liven up the night here girls? Have you had anything yet, Liza?"

The toddler chuckled. "A little..."

The rocker shook her head with a grin. "I suppose we've got to catch up then!" She waved over to the bartender. "I'd fancy a Bloody Mary tonight. What about you, Valorie?"

"Or-Orgasm, please."

"Of course." Monica placed their order, then dipped her hands into her pockets.

"You know, Valorie, the more I think about it, you and I are very much alike."

Val crossed her arms on the counter. "How so?"

"For starters..." The foreign girl folded her hands together. Liza rested her head in her hand and grinned. "You and I are both afraid of similar things. A fear of the unknown."

Val squinted. "How do you know what I-I'm afraid of?"

"Well, isn't it obvious?!" Monica scoffed. "You clearly hesitated when offered to have a drink with us tonight. I don't take offense of course, but by now you most certainly understand that we are not out to hurt you."

Fearful, Val looked over to the bartender. Monica went on.

"If I can be frank, my intention is the opposite. I seek to help you. We both do."

Eliza nodded cheerfully. Monica continued.

"There are many injustices in our world. In my mind, one of our greatest injustices is inequality. Inequality among men and women."

Val listened, suspicious of the direction this conversation was headed.

"I believe I've found a way to resolve this issue. But, for the sake of women everywhere, we all need to be brave.

Monica and Val turned their heads to two full cocktails when they arrived on the counter. The former played around with her lemon before taking a quick sip. Val resisted scoffing down her glass and paused after a few seconds.

"So, Miss Valorie, what do you say about our little cause?" Monica picked up her lemon and squeezed it into her drink. "Does it fancy your interest?"

Val found herself looking down at the counter.

"I-I... can't say."

"I see." Monica nodded quietly, then took another sip. Val seized this as an opportunity to drink a little more of her cocktail. She was already starting to feel buzzed.

"Perhaps you need a little convincing."

Val examined her glass. She was more than halfway finished. She told herself she'd stay just a few seconds longer before heading out the door.

"W-What do you have in mind?"

Monica traced her finger around the rim of her Bloody Mary. "You'll realize it, sooner or later. It's only a matter of time."

Val didn't know how to react to her comment, but she felt something bad was coming. She swallowed down some more of her Orgasm, then pushed away her stool.

"Thank you for the drink, Monica. It was a pleasure meeting you, Eliza." She stood up. "I've got somewhere I need to be now."

"Leaving so soon?" Monica stood up alongside her. "We just got here, love."

"Sorry, I've got someone waiting for me." Val picked up her suitcase. "Maybe we can have drinks again some time."

Monica smiled. "Of course." She stepped forward and gave Val a light hug. "It was most certainly a pleasure. Thank you for spending time with us."

When she stepped away, she grabbed Val by the hand. "I'm sure we'll see each other again very soon."

Val tried to genuinely smile back this time. "Yeah, I think so too."

The metalhead quickly slipped something onto Val's finger. Val's suitcase dropped to the floor with a loud thud.

✳✳✳

Val woke up on the torn-up sofa in her former apartment. She stared at the dust wafting in the sunlight by her window. She couldn't remember the last time she cleaned the place.

"Good morning, sweetheart."

Her eyes opened wide. She sat up excitedly, looking around the room for a person.

"Sleep well?"

Val stood and looked behind her sofa. She jolted into her bedroom and searched her bathroom. She couldn't find anyone.

"Hello?" That voice sounded familiar. She darted into her kitchen and grabbed the largest knife from the counter. Her heart raced. "Who's there?"

"Don't you recognize me, Val?" The voice giggled. "How could you forget your best friend?"

Tears welled in Val's eyes. She told her heart not to believe it. "You're not her." She pointed the knife out in front of her. "You're not real."

"Of course I am." The front door of her apartment opened wide on its own. "Come see for yourself."

Val hesitated. As her hands began trembling, she noticed a white ring on her finger. It looked very similar to one from last night.

She hurriedly tossed the knife to her couch and twisted the ring. She pulled as hard as she could to no avail. Missy was right. There's no easy way out of a nightmare.

She picked up the knife off her sofa and thought about what happened in the bar with the two girls she met. She mulled over every detail of their conversation. What did they want from her and how did they get the ring?

Val needed this to be over fast. She decided she'd rather be homeless than live inside her head.

She looked at her reflection in the knife and breathed in, breathed out. She told herself to be prepared for anything. It was easier said than done.

She walked out the front door and closed it behind her. She noticed footprints on the stairs leading up to the roof. They were gray like ash.

Val followed them to the roof. Before opening the door to the deck, she looked through the window to see if anyone was waiting for her. No one was there.

She opened the door hesitantly and tiptoed her way outside. The waning sunlight painted a warm picture across the long, winding sky. Under normal circumstances, Val would have been in awe.

"I'm here, honey." The voice returned. "Don't you see me?"

Val was losing patience. She yelled, "Stop messing with me! You're not real!"

"Look above you."

The homeless girl gripped onto her knife tighter than before. "No."

"Valorie…" The voice paused. "Please, just give me a chance."

Val looked up and noticed the night quickly swallow the sunlight. Dozens of stars began glimmering as the nighttime blanket unfolded. She quickly looked back down.

"Do you remember when we used to watch the stars together, Val?"

The orphan rubbed her eyes and pointed her weapon out further than before. "Who are you?"

Ignoring Val's comment, the voice continued. "We were lucky to see two or three at a time. It seemed so silly, living in the city and everything. But we always liked to do it anyway."

Val didn't know how to respond. Her throat was drying up. The night had almost entirely replaced the sunlit sky.

"Look how many stars are up there now, Val. They're watching us, all the way from a place high above the clouds."

Val shook her head. Teardrops slowly cascaded down her cheeks. "Please… stop…."

"I'm sorry I'm not with you. I wish I could change things." The voice paused as if lost in thought, then went on. "But I'll be watching. I'll always be watching over you."

Val collapsed to her knees. She sobbed. "Mom… I miss you."

"Wherever you go, Valorie, I'll be there." The voice chuckled. "Even inside your head."

The bartender-in-training bent over in anguish. She could barely see beyond her tears. She wished her mother was back to take away all the pain. She wished she wasn't a complete fuckup.

Val cried and cried. More stars appeared overhead, as if they were trying to console her. It was finally time she let it all out. It was time for her to move on from the torture.

When Val had no tears left to cry, she looked up at the stars and admired them for a while. She wished she could be out there. She told herself that she'd go someday.

Something shattered on the rooftop a few feet away. It sounded like glass.

Val wiped her face and steadied her breathing. She stood up and walked over to the debris. Tiny pieces of mirror lay strewn in one spot.

The dreamer gripped her knife a little tighter. Something was coming. She whispered to herself, "Be brave."

Seconds later, another mirror crashed onto the rooftop. Val jumped back, swinging the knife up from her side and pointing it out in front of her.

She looked over to the only doorway and walked back towards it, monitoring her surroundings for signs of zombies.

Val made it to her exit safely and opened the door. She checked again to see if anyone was following. No one was there.

As soon as the door shut, she peered out the window from an angle. She wasn't going to take any chances. She clung onto her weapon with both hands, ready to strike at a moment's notice.

With her anguish now subsided, Val felt she desperately needed to free herself from her mind. She needed to breathe again in the real world.

Val winced when the third mirror shattered on the rooftop. Less than a minute later, a fourth arrived. A fifth and sixth mirror exploded shortly after, then came the rain.

Dozens of mirrors came crashing down on the rooftop, each splintering into thousands of minuscule glass fragments. Val looked on from behind the door's window, thinking about the city that lay behind her building.

Several minutes passed before the mirrors stopped falling. When the onslaught was over, Val glimpsed at the sky from the protection of her stairwell. The stars were gone.

She then looked down on the thousands of shards on the roof. At the center of the chaos, the pieces began swirling like a whirlpool.

The spiral grew rapidly, eventually taking over the entire area. Val stared in horror, thinking the broken mirror pieces were summoning something she didn't want to face.

The pile grew in the middle, then detonated high into the sky. Val cowered behind the door, afraid of getting caught in the blast.

When the debris settled, she stayed scrunched up in the corner of the stairwell. She didn't want to see what now rested beyond that door.

"Valorie, Valorie, have you finally grown a pair?"

Val's eyes widened. She jutted her knife out and looked down the stairwell. Monica's plan was coming to fruition.

The homeless girl yelled. "What the hell do you want from me?!"

The mysterious girl giggled. "Quite riled up, are we?"

Val couldn't tell where Monica's voice was coming from. She scanned every corner, but didn't dare look outside the window.

"Consider this a character-building exercise, love. A means of facing your fears head-on."

Beads of sweat started rolling down Val's forehead. She had an idea of who was waiting outside. She didn't want to face her.

"You can thank us later."

"You tricked me!" Val clenched her ringed hand. "I can't believe you fucking tricked me!"

"We'll talk later, dear." The orphan could picture Monica smiling from wherever she was. "For now, you've got a mother to entertain."

Val's heart sank. She looked down at the knife in her hand. She couldn't tell herself to be brave anymore. That energy was gone now.

She slowly backed up to the door. Breath by breath, she rotated her head to the window. She looked out and saw her dead mother standing in the middle of a valley of mirrors.

The knife shook in Val's hand. The homeless girl closed her eyes and tried to erase her thoughts.

She whispered again to herself. "T-This is all... inside my head."

The figment of imagination waiting for Val outside was wearing her mother's favorite summer dress. The orphan missed seeing it on her.

Val slowly tilted her head to the window again. She looked at her mother's face for the first time in what seemed like forever. She was smiling at her.

Instinctively, Val turned the door's handle. She pushed hard to move the pieces of glass blocking it.

She closed the door behind her, standing in a glassless half-circle. Her mother extended her hand and motioned her daughter to come over.

Val breathed in, breathed out and whispered again. "This is… inside my head." She dragged her feet a few inches forward.

The valley of broken mirrors parted, as if enticing Val to run to her mother with open arms. The suspicious orphan stuck her knife out in front of her instead, pointing it wearily at her mother.

She gulped, then summoned the courage to speak. "W-Who are you?"

Her mother didn't reply. She clasped her hands together and continued to smile.

Val continued dragging her feet forward uneasily.

She inched closer, trying her best to steady the knife in her hand. Her mother stood there, motionless and silent.

"Inside my head. This is… inside my head." Val needed the encouragement. She couldn't keep her sanity without it.

Once Val was a few feet away, her mother opened her arms wide. A hug to welcome her daughter home.

Val stopped. She examined her mother's rose-colored fingernails, platform shoes and long frilly dress. Every beauty mark and wrinkle on her face was just as she remembered. Her smile was just as bright too.

The shaky knife slowly retreated to Val's side. "M-Mom?"

Val stepped in closer. The mother continued beaming, stretching out her arms to greet her.

The homeless girl raised her other hand to touch her mom's face. She missed her so much.

Val tried to hold back more tears. "Is that r-really you, mom?"

She was close now. The figment seized its chance.

Val's mom pounced. Her daughter's eyes widened. The knife fell to the rooftop.

Suddenly, Val was being choked to death inside her nightmare.

As the light gradually faded from her eyes, she couldn't help but think she deserved everything that happened to her.

The world needs less fuckups.

A shotgun barked into the night sky. Val collapsed to the floor and gasped for air. A blonde blur darted along the edge of the rooftop.

Val looked up in time to witness a fist sock her mother in the head, sending her flying to the edge of the building.

Chrissy stood triumphantly in front of her with fists clenched, aching to land another blow. Sissy and Missy landed beside her, the former with a shotgun over her shoulder and the latter equipped with a shard-laden shield.

The redhead turned around halfway, stuck her thumb up and grinned. "We just saved you from an extremely painful death! Yay!"

Val took several more breaths before shouting, "Why are you… here?!"

"Don't worry, Valorie." Chrissy kept staring ahead, expecting some sort of retaliation. "We're here to help."

"I expect no less of you, Miss Chrissy."

Shadows danced on the glass-littered rooftop as Val's ill-intentioned mother struggled to find the upper body strength to stand.

"You should know that your habit of interfering with noble causes is nauseating."

Val's mind finally made the connection. She wobbled to her feet and yelled at the trio.

"There's this girl named Monica! She tricked me into wearing a ring! She set me up—"

"We know." Chrissy eyes followed the shadows as they tossed frantically across the flat surface in front of the girls. "She's a fucking bitch."

The dark shapes rushed forward. Sissy shot several as they approached, but one zipped behind her. A shadowy figure rose from the silhouette and launched itself at Val.

Chrissy exclaimed, "Valorie, out of the way!"

Val jumped back just as the pigtailed gun freak unleashed a round. Coils of shadow untangled themselves in the air where the apparition once was.

The former prospect looked down at her body to make sure she wasn't caught in the blast. That was a close one.

Her interviewer extended a hand. "Sorry about that. Siss can get a little carried away sometimes."

Chrissy flashed a stern look at her redheaded employee. The arms aficionado put up a peace sign wearily. Missy shook her head.

Val accepted Chrissy's help and stood up again. She looked over at the hunched woman at the rooftop's edge. A tinge of sadness swept through her.

"Siss, lend me a pistol."

In a second, the gun-toting maniac flipped a handgun into her free hand. She bobbed it to her boss, who in turn laid it in Val's hand.

The dreamer looked at the weapon wide-eyed, then looked into Chrissy's eyes.

"I can't—"

"It's your nightmare, Valorie." The blonde folded Val's hands around the gun. "You need to finish this on your own."

"You're quite despicable, love." A large shadowy shark fin appeared and rotated around the quartet in the clearing. "Why not let Miss Valorie quench her fears on her terms?"

"You set her up to die." Chrissy followed the fin as it circled her crew. "You did it to satisfy your goddamn agenda."

Monica chuckled. "Did you not put her through a similar atrocity? Fling her headfirst into a nightmare of your choosing? We have different ways of interviewing, love. My methodology just happens to be more sensible."

For the first time, Val saw veins appear on Chrissy's temples. The blonde clenched her fists once more and crouched. "I don't understand you."

Monica laughed from the shadows again. "You will, dear."

The shark fin sunk into the rooftop. Dozens of shadowy hands launched along its path, palms stretched wide to snatch the girls below.

Chrissy picked Val up by the collar of her jean jacket. "Go!"

She rocketed the homeless girl over the onslaught. Val shrieked before slamming down hard on her back. Bits of glass dug into her hair, legs and shoulders as she skidded to a halt.

When she looked over to the trio, it was gone. She glanced at the gun in her hand.

Her injured mother kneeled a short distance away. Blood oozed from her nostrils and seeped onto her favorite summer dress.

✳✳✳

Chrissy, Missy and Sissy fell endlessly in a vacuum. The blonde caught Missy by the shoulder, then extended a hand to Sissy. The redhead pretended not to see it. She smiled from ear to ear, as if expecting this all along.

Her employer yelled, "Sissy! Take my hand!"

The gun freak looked over with a crazed expression on her face. She dug inside her skirt and pulled out her alcohol.

Missy's eyes widened. "Are you shitting me? Don't you fucking dare!"

"Siss, Missy is right! It's too dangerous!"

Sissy unscrewed the cap and guzzled down the rest of her liquid. She tossed the tin behind her when done, then exclaimed, "I'm fucking hammered!"

Chrissy kicked toward the joker while still hanging onto Missy. She caught one of her hands and looked her associate in the eye.

"That's enough, Siss! You're being too reckless!"

Sissy tee-heed in response and snapped the fingers in her free hand. A dozen sawed-off shotguns spun around them. She pushed away Chrissy's grip and dived ahead.

"Cover your butts!"

Blondie pleaded one last time. "Siss, stop!"

The redhead looked behind her and winked. "But it's so much fun!"

She waved the shotguns neatly around her and grasped the closest. She aimed it straight down and laughed maniacally.

When Sissy pulled the trigger, the other guns busted their loads simultaneously, shooting off into every direction. Holes punctured the fabric of Monica's void.

A blinding light rippled below the girls and returned them to the rooftop.

When Chrissy's eyes adjusted, she spotted Sissy standing over her, shotgun pointed at a woman laying atop a carpet of glass.

"That's enough, Siss!" Chrissy stood up and lowered her employee's weapon. "I think you've caused enough trouble today."

Monica coughed up blood while gripping the holes in her stomach. She struggled to crane her neck and address the trio nearby.

"It's not… over…"

Missy conjured an ax into her hand. "What do we do, Chris?"

The blonde stared at Monica's gory, glass-embedded body for a few seconds before replying. "Take her ring. Let's put an end to this."

The smoker nodded hesitantly. "You got it."

She stepped carefully over the broken glass to reach Monica. Chrissy looked to Val. The dreamer was watching them, mouth agape. Fisticuffs smiled her way.

Val half-grinned in return, then turned back to her mother. The handgun rattled by her side.

She tried focusing on her breathing. One breath in, one breath out. The gun in her hand didn't feel any lighter.

The door to the rooftop banged wide open. Everyone looked over. A girl with hair drills stood in the frame.

Chrissy squinted, then yelled, "Who are you?"

The young girl didn't reply. Instead, she raised a hand out and pointed it like a gun. Her body brightened like a light bulb.

Monica chuckled and whispered, "Welcome to the party."

Bursts of electricity surged off Eliza as she aimed her finger at Missy. Sissy shook her shotgun free from Chrissy's grasp and focused it on the girl. Blondie screamed.

"Sissy, enough!"

The redhead giggled. She pulled her trigger, but the short girl dodged. As the door hinge fell to the ground, Eliza changed her target.

A bolt of lightning rushed from her index finger into Sissy's retina.

The redhead collapsed, smoke billowing from her eye socket. Chrissy caught her before she fell on glass.

The teen seized her chance and jolted across the rooftop toward Missy, expertly avoiding every shard on the surface. The stoner swung her ax once Eliza was close, but missed. Electro grabbed Missy from behind and unleashed a shockwave, flinging her to the stairwell.

Eliza picked up Monica carefully. She looked over to Val and smiled playfully.

"See you later, crybaby!"

Her body brightened again before she catapulted with Monica into the night sky. She darted along other rooftops before disappearing completely.

Val stood wide-eyed, unsure of what happened. She looked over to Chrissy, who stared into Sissy's face incredulously.

The blonde yelled. "Valorie!"

The orphan froze.

"End this! Right now!"

Chrissy stood up with Sissy in her arms and turned. Tears welled in her eyes.

"Please…"

Val looked down at the gun again, then turned to her mother. She tried hard to breathe.

Chapter 6
Yachts 'N Thots

Val woke up on a hard surface, the sun beating down mercilessly on her face. She shielded her eyes with her hands and lifted her head.

She was sitting alone on the deck of a cruise ship. The sea over the railings ebbed and flowed in blood red. Clue two she was not in the real world. Clue one was being too broke to afford a cruise trip.

The dreamer stood up in alarm. Then she remembered where she was.

She breathed in, breathed out. A gentle breeze stirred around her and a touch of cold kissed her feet. She noticed she was wearing nothing but a white two-piece swimsuit. Her cheeks lit up.

Val looked around for a towel to cover herself with and found one laying on a chaise. She wrapped it around her torso before someone appeared from around the ship's funnel.

Missy walked over wearing a dark blue bandeau bikini set. She didn't look very amused.

"Where'd you get the towel?"

Val turned and scanned the entire deck. "I think I took the last one. Sorry."

The sword-bearer scoffed and waved a dagger into her hand. She crouched and started carving her name into the floor.

Val crossed her arms and looked over to the strange ocean. She tried to distract herself from thinking about what happened the other night.

After a few minutes, someone touched down on the wood from behind. The homeless girl turned and saw Chrissy proudly standing in a yellow one-piece. The blonde smiled her way.

"Get here in one piece, Valorie?"

Val returned the grin. "Yeah, no worries here." Aside from the two-piece.

"Excellent." Chrissy stretched out her hands to the sun. "Beautiful day for a tan, isn't it?"

"Can we get this whole training thing over with?" Missy stood up and tossed her dagger into the water. "I feel like I'm naked."

Her employer chuckled. "Understandable, Miss. Valorie, let's talk for a bit. Then we'll move on with the show."

Val followed Chrissy to a chaise and sat beside her. Missy walked to the ship's railing and twirled harpoons into her hands. She launched them at the fish below.

"Let me start by saying I'm super glad you decided to join the team. You know your way around cocktails and your skills are definitely going to give us an edge in battle."

The blonde paused and looked down. After a few seconds, she folded her hands and looked back up at Val. "Maybe it wasn't the best idea to toss you in a nightmare headfirst. I'm sorry about that."

Val nodded and looked away. "I-It's fine."

"It's not. Neither is what happened the other night." Chrissy rubbed her thumbs together. "Hopefully we won't be seeing much of Monica anymore."

"Who is she?" Val blurted out the question before mulling it over in her head. She nervously adjusted the towel around her body, half-expecting her new boss not to answer.

Chrissy sighed loudly. "Well, to be honest, she used to work for us."

Val crossed her arms. She looked down at the deck and noticed her reflection. The blonde continued.

"One day, when the rest of us weren't looking, she infiltrated our headquarters and stole a handful of rings. She was gone right after that."

Chrissy tilted her head up at the innocent clouds above. "We see her now and then, but never fight or anything. We just yell at each other, maybe exchange a few swear words. The other night..." She took a deep breath. "She was different."

Chrissy paused again, leaned back and rested her head in her hands. "To be frank, I can't tell if she's confident or desperate."

Val looked up at Chrissy and asked another question. "What about the other girl? Eliza, I think?"

"No idea." Boss lady shrugged. "She's dangerous, no doubt about it."

The new hire closed her eyes and breathed in, breathed out. Chrissy wrapped her arm around her.

"Don't worry, Valorie." She smiled. "Everything's gonna be alright."

At that moment, Val wondered if she changed her mind due to desperation, pity or a blend of the two.

"Anyway." Chrissy straightened her back and crossed her arms. "Now's the fun part. It's time to become a magical alcohol girl!"

The girl in training grinned weakly.

"First thing's first!" The blonde hopped up and clapped her hands. "We need to figure out your class."

"My... class?"

"Yup!" Chrissy talked as she pranced over to Missy. "There are three types of classes: Emitters, Conjurers and Specials."

She grabbed Missy's shoulder just after the short-haired girl furiously launched another harpoon below. "Miss here is a Conjurer, which means she can materialize objects from thin air. Siss is the same."

Chrissy whispered something into Missy's ear, then continued. "The girls from the other day are Emitters, which means they can manipulate the energy around them and transform it into some kind of elemental power."

Val stood up and adjusted her towel again. "What's your class, then?"

Blondie smiled. "I'm not a Conjurer or an Emitter, so I'm part of the rare Special class." She stretched her arms above her head. "I may not be able to conjure grenades or lightning or whatever, but I sure pack a punch!"

Val nodded, then wondered what trials the girls were going to put her through next. "S-So how do we find my class?"

"It's easy!" Chrissy pointed Missy to the opposite end of the deck. The smoker waved a hammer into her hand and walked over, snickering as she passed Val. "We're going to spar with you!"

The homeless girl audibly gulped.

"I-I can't."

"You've got to stop saying that, Valorie." Chrissy winked and turned her back. She walked to the other end of the deck, then yelled, "Don't worry! We won't hurt you!"

Val sincerely doubted that. A bead of sweat rolled down her cheek.

"Let us know when you're ready!"

The dreamer didn't know how to spar, let alone prepare for a sparring match. Once again, she asked herself what the hell she got herself into.

After a few minutes of raking her mind for a strategy, she shakily gave Chrissy a thumbs up.

Her boss grinned. She cupped her hands over her mouth and shouted, "Missy! Attack when I say go!"

Val's eyes grew wide. She hoped she wouldn't get walloped too terribly. She held on tight to the towel around her.

"Ready?!"

Val closed her eyes and breathed in, breathed out.

"Go!"

Chrissy and Missy pounced, the former clenching a fist in midair and the latter winding up her hammer.

Val ducked as soon as she heard Chrissy plant her feet next to her. Missy swung before she realized what Val was up to.

The blonde caught the hammer a few inches from her face. Val cowered on the floor, shaking nervously with her hands over her head.

Chrissy laughed. "Clever! You were gonna have us take out each other, huh?" She extended a hand to Val. "Maybe we're being a bit too aggressive. Scaring the class out of you might not work."

Val grabbed onto Chrissy's hand and stood up. She offered a suggestion. "M-Maybe we can do a one-on-one session? I've never actually fought anyone before, s-so… that might be helpful."

Bossy crossed her arms. "Sure, I don't see why not. Maybe we can—"

A strong wind caught the girls by surprise. It unwrapped Val's towel and flung to the other side of the ship. Val reached out a hand.

"No!"

The wind obediently blew back into her direction, tossing the towel straight into her face.

When Val removed the towel from her head, she saw sparkles in Chrissy's eyes.

"W-What's wrong?"

Chrissy bounced in place. "I think we just found your magical alcohol girl power!"

Val put on a confused expression while wrapping the towel around her again. "What do you mean?"

Missy facepalmed. "Dude, you just controlled the goddamn wind."

The newbie replayed the last minute in her mind. "I didn't—"

"Missy!" Chrissy grabbed her associate's shoulder. Missy looked back in surprise. "I knew this girl was a keeper. We've finally got an Emitter!"

Val took a step back. "I'm not sure I r-really did that."

With a blank expression, Missy seized Chrissy's hands and rested them by her side. She walked uncomfortably close to Val and, without saying anything, pulled the towel off her. She crunched it into a ball and hurled it over the railing.

Val reached out instinctively.

"Why—?!"

The towel ball unfurled and sped back to Val through a brief gust of wind. It landed by her bare feet. She stared at it with her mouth open.

"Do you believe it now, dipshit?"

Val picked up the towel, looking at it incredulously. Chrissy walked over and spun around on her heel.

"I can't believe we found your power so quickly!" She wrapped her arm around Val again. "We're going to have a lot of fun together!"

Though still mostly consumed by her confusion, Val felt something warm stir inside her. For the first time in a while, she thought she felt a sense of accomplishment.

It didn't last long.

The ship shook, quickly leaning in opposite directions and causing the girls to lose their balance. As chaises fell overboard, Val looked to the ocean. Huge blood-red waves bobbed dangerously close to their vessel.

Chrissy grabbed her hand.

"This way!"

Val dropped her towel and ran with her new boss and Missy to a set of double doors beneath the bridge. Chrissy opened the doors and motioned her employees inside, then slammed the doors behind her.

As they caught their breaths, Chrissy raised a finger.

"One last thing!" She smiled, apparently unperturbed by the rapid change of events. Something grumbled from the stairwell at the other end of the hall.

Blondie produced a liquor tin from her one-piece and offered it to Val. "To maintain our magical alcohol girl powers, we need to constantly be hammered. Drink up!"

Val took the container. "A-Are you serious?"

Chrissy put her hands on her hips proudly as the ship sank into another direction. "Yup! Give it a try. I think you'll like what you taste!"

The new hire unscrewed the cap and put her lips on the opening. She sipped the tin for a second, then glanced at Chrissy with her eyebrows raised.

"Or-Orgasm? How'd you know?"

"I noticed it the night you stiffed us." She winked. "Drink some more! It'll come in handy."

Val looked away, slightly embarrassed. She drank a little more in silence.

Missy yawned as the ship tilted again. "Are we, like, gonna fuck shit up eventually or…?"

Chrissy rolled her eyes. "As you can see, Valorie, *some* people are getting impatient." She smirked at Missy. The smoker folded her hands and turned around. "Before we go down those stairs, do you have any questions?"

As Val fastened her tin inside her waistband, she grew nervous. Her employer had yet to say how or when exactly she was going to get paid.

"I-I don't mean to sound rude or anything, b-but," Val clasped her hands around her back and looked to the metallic floor. "W-When can I expect my first paycheck?"

Her face brightened. Chrissy slapped herself on the head.

"Duh! Totally forgot about that. You should get your first check in two weeks." The blonde fluffed up her hair. "I'll hand you an envelope from the RBA—Restaurant and Bar Association. They're the ones that pay us to do what we do!"

Val nodded. "Got it. Thank you." She felt relieved to get that detail out of the way. For a brief moment, she imagined herself inside her old apartment again.

"Alrighty!" The boss lady stretched her arms up and rotated her hips. "Are we ready to end this thing?"

"I've been ready for fucking forever." Missy waved a falchion into her hand. "Let's get this shit over with already."

Chrissy looked at Val. "You ready, newbie?"

Val breathed in, breathed out. "Yeah, let's do this."

Chrissy grinned wide. "Perfect! I'll take the lead."

The blonde jogged over to the staircase. Val followed close behind, and Missy kept an eye on their rear.

They climbed down one flight after another for what seemed like a couple of minutes. Val wondered how a cruise ship could have so many stairs. Then she remembered this was a dream.

After a while, Chrissy stopped for a drink. As she sipped from her tin, she said, "I forgot to mention before, Valorie, but this is important."

Val looked at her new boss inquisitively while Missy took a second to replenish herself, too. In a serious tone, fisticuffs continued.

"Never drink more than you should—only a little bit of alcohol at a time suffices. You may be tempted to drink more for a boost." Chrissy looked to the wall with a faraway expression. "But that usually just leads to trouble. Trouble for your team and, well, yourself."

The dreamer knew Chrissy was referring to Sissy. She stared at the landing, unsure of what to say.

"Anyway." Chrissy stashed her alcohol. "Let's continue, shall we?"

Val nodded. They hurried down another series of staircases, the ship tossing haphazardly as they made their way to the basement. Finally, they came across another set of double doors.

Chrissy motioned to them. "Feeling lucky, Valorie?"

Val's body shuddered when she remembered the noise she heard when they first arrived inside. All her senses told her to avoid discovering whatever rested on the other side.

"Yeah. I-I'll go first." She desperately wanted to feel brave, especially after what happened the other night.

Chrissy nodded approvingly. "Be our guest."

Val gripped her hands around the door's handles. She listened for noise, but couldn't hear anything. After some hesitation, she told herself to grow a pair.

The doors to the ship's basement were thrown wide open. A gigantesque, naked baby sat in front of Val with its back turned, voraciously feeding on what seemed like a huge stack of dollar bills.

Chrissy and Missy followed close behind the new hire, staring at the oversized infant with confused expressions.

Missy grimaced. "What the… fuck?"

Bossy chuckled. "Well, here's something you don't see every day."

The creature stuffed its mouth with another fistful of money. Val took a step back, doubting if she had the courage for this line of work.

Chrissy grabbed her shoulder. "Don't worry, this should be an easy one. Look around." She pointed at the metallic radiators, pipes and boilers that lay strewn across the room. "If you can knock that thing unconscious by slamming it into a hard surface, we'll take care of the rest for you."

Val examined her surroundings, planning her strategy of attack. The baby stopped chewing before she could find a solid course of action.

The monster threw its weight and rotated on its side. It pushed up and yelled, then began crawling toward the magical alcohol girls with a disgruntled expression on its face.

Missy side-jumped quickly behind a boiler. Chrissy patted Val on the back. "Knock 'em dead—literally!"

She jumped to the other side of the basement, leaving her new employee alone with a rampaging baby fast approaching.

Val breathed rapidly. Her heart raced a thousand times a minute. Her mind told her that she couldn't do it. She closed her eyes.

She focused her consciousness on every bit of air in, every bit of air out. She noticed how her lungs expanded as she inhaled and how her lips moved as she exhaled.

Val loved the stillness to it. Even in the face of horror, she can choose to find peace.

She pictured the wind wrapping itself around her, holding her like her mother used to on their rooftop at night. She imagined it spinning around her like a vortex, pushing back the voices inside her head. For a brief moment, all of the negativity inside her vanished.

The wind was going to take good care of her.

A current blasted through the double doors from which she came, zooming over Val's head and slamming the infant directly in its face.

The baby gulped and lifted its head back abruptly, accidentally crashing it into a large pipe above.

It fell to the floor with a thud. The stream of air dissipated. Val breathed out and opened her eyes. Somehow, she was alive.

Missy emerged from her hiding spot first with her mouth wide open. "How the… fuck?"

Val smiled nervously. "Beginner's luck, I guess?"

"Luck? That was pure talent!" Chrissy skipped to her two associates. "I can't believe you managed to pull that off! I mean, I didn't doubt you or anything, but that was seriously impressive."

Val looked to her feet, feeling embarrassed, relieved and still somewhat uneasy. "Are you guys, um, going to take care of the rest now?"

Chrissy slapped her head again. "Oh yeah. Duh! Miss, can you finish it off for us please?"

Missy snarled and traded her falchion for the hammer from before. "Yeah, whatever."

As the stoner walked over to the baby, the blonde moved in close to Val and grasped her hands.

"I really can't understate how impressed I am with you. Day one and you're already killing it!"

Val's face grew red. "T-Thank you." She shuffled her feet. "But I've still got a lot to learn."

"And learn you shall!" Chrissy squeezed Val's hands. "This is the start of a beautiful relationship. I can feel it!"

The warmth that Val felt earlier returned to her. For the first time since she lost her home, she genuinely smiled.

"Me too."

Chapter 7
864 Mesmerizing Inches

The only television in the room farted its obesity into motion picture.

"You see doctor, recently my parents divorced. I've been feeling useless throughout the whole experience, and it's making me depressed. Given my situation, how often do you recommend I trim my bush?"

Val had grown accustomed to daytime programming's desperate attempts to remain relevant. She leaned her slightly hungover head back on the torn-up sofa in her apartment, wrinkling up her black and red uniform. A dozen Chinese food pails lay open on her kitchen counter.

"So, are you used to constantly being hammered yet?"

Missy leaned against the wall, inhaling a bag of barbeque-flavored potato chips with her orange-colored fingertips.

"Kind of." It had been a few weeks since Missy begrudgingly became Val's roommate. Unsurprisingly, the stoner got kicked out of her last place for smoking too much weed.

Despite initial concerns, Val didn't find her new living situation too much of a headache most of the time. Plus, splitting the rent two ways helped ease her anxiety (and purse).

Val closed her eyes. "You're taking the night off, right?"

Missy slinked to the floor. "Yeah. I worked every day last week."

Val nodded. "I understand. You need your rest."

The junkie finished her chips, crunched her bag into a ball and tossed it into the corner. She dug into her jeans pocket and pulled out a blunt and a lighter. Val glanced over.

"I told you no smoking—"

"It's just tobacco, whore."

Missy stuck the wand into her mouth and ignited. Val grinned and closed her eyes again.

The foul-mouthed delinquent took a few tokes before asking a question. "Are you going to the hospital with Chris tonight?"

Val crossed her legs together. "Yeah. Sissy should be happy."

Missy sucked on her blunt and held her breath for a minute before exhaling. "Tell her I still think she's a bitch."

Val placed her hands beneath her head. "Noted."

***

Val and Chrissy arrived at the redhead's room not long before visiting hours were up, slightly buzzed in preparation for the night ahead.

"Aw shit, my bitches are back!"

Sissy bounced excitedly on her bed as the pair smiled and walked their way over.

Chrissy squealed with delight. "Siss! How have you been, girl?!"

The erratic gunslinger had mostly returned to her hyperactive self. An eyepatch holed up the place where her left pupil used to be.

"Great! The docs say I'm getting released soon!"

Chrissy sat down next to her associate on the bed. Val preferred to stand. "That's fantastic news! Don't you think so, Valorie?"

Val had to remind herself not to stare at Sissy's injury each time they visited. "Y-Yeah! Of course! I'm so glad you're coming back soon, Sissy."

She thought back to when the pigtailed patient almost shot her. She had her misgivings about Sissy, but told herself to remain optimistic.

"I can't wait for this team to be back in action." Chrissy clasped her hands. "Val's made so much progress, Siss. She can even freaking fly now!"

Sissy's eye opened wide. "Whoa." She turned to Val. "You serious?"

Val took a step back, slightly embarrassed. "Y-Yeah, but I'm not perfect at it yet."

"Can you imagine?!" Chrissy spread her arms out. "One day we're going to fly side by side, shooting rifles, tossing daggers and throwing hands from way above the stratosphere. I'm so hyped!"

The newest hire scratched the back of her head. "I-I haven't really figured out the best techniques yet but yeah, that would be fun."

Sissy started vibrating in place again. "Cool! I can't wait, I can't wait, I can't wait!"

"Me too!" Chrissy beamed, then stared down at the floor. She let a few seconds pass in silence before speaking again.

"We haven't run into Monica and Eliza yet, by the way." She squeezed Sissy's leg and looked her in the face. "Whenever they do show up again, we're definitely gonna need you around. You're indispensable, Siss."

Unperturbed by the mention of her assailant, Sissy saluted her employer. "Roger that, homie!"

Chrissy chuckled and stood. "Anyway, I hate to cut our visit so short, but we've got to get going now. Our first stop tonight is the 'Choking Chicken.'"

Patchy shook her head. "Love that place."

The boss lady stretched her back and yawned. "Do you need anything before we leave? Soda?"

Sissy reached inside her pillowcase and grabbed something, then responded. "Nope! I've got plenty of rubbers for tonight."

Chrissy crossed her arms and smirked. "I'm glad you're keeping yourself busy. Valorie, shall we depart?"

Val nodded. "Yeah! Just one m-more thing."

The newbie reached into her pocket and pulled out her old PSZ. She handed it to Sissy.

"I t-thought you might want to play some video games while you f-finish up your recovery." She shrugged. "There's this cool s-sci-fi game in there that might give you inspiration for more g-guns."

The redhead grabbed the handheld with mouth agape. "Vidya… gaems?"

"That's brilliant, Valorie!" Chrissy jumped in place. "Imagine all the cool laser guns and blasters you can whip out after a few hours of playing video games! It's going to be so epic!"

Sissy tilted her head and stared at herself in the PSZ's reflection. Slowly, a smile grew across her face.

***

Blonde and brunette sat atop empty paint cans plastered with tetanus in an abandoned alleyway behind one of their routine bars. Maggots, bronies and other urban scum festered in broken beer bottles and piss-stained drainage pipes. Some poor inebriated soul shimmied up a nearby lamppost, swiveled off a light bulb and ran away in the dark.

Val raised an eyebrow. "Should we—?"

"Nah, let him have fun with himself."

The airbender shifted on her can and closed her eyes. She breathed in, breathed out. It helped her prepare for her shift.

Chrissy stood up on her can and looked through the window of the 'Choking Chicken' behind them. She sat back down and folded her arms.

"Looks like our friend still has a little more life left in him. We'll slip on our rings soon."

Val nodded, eyes still closed. "You got it."

Her boss looked at her and smiled. "Hey, do you mind if I asked you a question?"

The new associate turned her head in surprise. "Y-Yeah, sure."

Chrissy shifted her seat. She stared at the ground as she spoke again. "Do you like your job?"

Val's face grew a little red. She folded her arms, too.

"You didn't accept my offer the first time around." The boss lady looked up. "I just want to make sure you're happy here."

The plain Jane didn't respond right away. Over the past few weeks, she managed to get her apartment back, forged a dysfunctional relationship with a person that used to intimidate her and found a friend in Chrissy. She couldn't remember the last time she ate ramen noodles or crackers.

To top it all off, she wasn't that terrible at being a magical alcohol girl.

Though the memory of her last dream with her mother still haunted her on occasion, Val couldn't say that her experience at her new job was less than mediocre. In fact, it excited her sometimes.

Val finally spoke up. "I'll be honest." She smiled at Chrissy. "It could be a lot worse."

Her boss grinned in return. "I'm so glad to hear that, Valorie. I really am."

Chrissy fluffed her hair and went on. "In case you were wondering, I meant what I said back there. I don't think Miss or Siss learned the ropes as fast as you." She lightly punched Val's shoulder. "You were born for this, girl!"

The Emitter's cheeks lit up. Maybe she really was where she belonged.

A group of dickheads cheered together from the bar behind the pair. Chrissy stood on her can and looked through the window. She laughed.

"You might want to see this."

Val tiptoed on her seat and took a peek. Inside, a half-naked man (bottoms down, of course) balanced a ping pong ball on his toe while hopping on a pogo stick. The cheese spray over his suit jacket and tie desperately tried to make him Superman.

Chrissy shook her head. "This is what cable does to people."

Val tried steadying her breathing as she rotated a ring in her pocket. She watched the drunk pogo away until he slipped on his tighty whities and fell carrot-first on the splintered wooden floor of the bar.

The blonde hopped off her can, whipped out her alcohol bottle and took a sip. Val did the same.

Chrissy stashed away her juice and revealed her yellow ring next. "Ready to get the night started, Valorie?"

The new hire nodded confidently while producing a white ring of her own. "I thought you'd never ask."

The two girls inserted themselves into a fucked-up fantasy.

***

Each skidooed out of computer monitors into a crowded space muddled with desolate cubicles, low-hanging ceiling fans and overturned stacks of paper. They stared down at their maid outfits as a pale fog rolled in.

Chrissy looked over at Val while holding the hem of her dress in disgust. "Well, I can't say I'm a fan of this guy."

Val giggled. "Yeah, his taste is definitely lacking."

Something titanic stomped outside and rumbled the entire room. Val rushed over to the broken window frame to investigate. An empty, apocalyptic cityscape greeted her there. Abandoned buildings and decimated streets were the only things she could see through the haze.

Chrissy grabbed Val's shoulder while looking outside herself. "Find anything interesting out there?"

Val scanned the overgrown roads for signs of life. She spotted a pair of massive footprints arching around an edifice in the distance.

The airbender gulped audibly and pointed. "Looks like we're up against something big."

Chrissy squinted to confirm, then nodded. "It won't be the first time. Let's climb for a better—"

A blast resounded from below. The duo leaned out the window frame and witnessed the first three floors of the adjacent building detonate. The edifice toppled toward the girls fast.

Val summoned courage with a deep breath. Without hesitation, she swung a fist forward and punched a hole of wind straight through the debris. Chrissy gripped onto her employee's free arm with a grin.

The boss lady kicked off with Val by her side, speeding through the cavity and flying high into the overcast sky. Val examined the loneliness of the city below as a part of it collapsed behind them.

They rolled to a stop on an empty gravel rooftop. As Val caught her breath, she couldn't help but notice how cold the air was. A bitter wind blew hair across her face.

Chrissy stretched her hamstrings while still on the ground. "What the hell was that all about?"

Val tossed her hair back and shook her head. "I don't know... but it's giving me a bad feeling."

Chrissy stood up tall and smiled at Val. "Well, whatever it is, we'll take care of it together."

Val grinned softly. She tried not to imagine the worst possible scenario. "Yeah, you're right."

"Of course I am!" The blonde walked over to the rooftop's iron railing and looked out at the city. "This is the best magical alcohol girl team I ever had, after all!"

A warmness stirred inside Val as she walked over to her boss and stared at the metropolis alongside her.

After a minute, Val looked over at Chrissy and asked, "Do you really mean that?"

Fisticuffs turned her head toward her associate and nodded. "Absolutely."

Val looked back out to the cityscape and folded her arms on the railing, feeling satisfied with where her journey had taken her so far. She was proud of the woman she had become after a few short weeks.

The wind whipped past her again. It didn't feel as harsh that time.

More buildings faintly crumbled far away. A circular shadow appeared behind the pair.

"Have you made up your mind yet, Miss Valorie?"

Chrissy rotated on her heels and clenched her fists. Val's eyes grew wide as she turned around slowly.

"What do you say about our cause?" Tiny black bubbles materialized on the rooftop and joined the circle. "Have you given it much thought?"

"Valorie is *not* joining your team, Monica." Chrissy arched her back and focused on the dark shape growing in front of her. "She has a happy career with us now."

"Is that so?" Monica's smirking human form arose from the circle. She wore a maid uniform similar to that of her former employer. "Do you care to elaborate, Valorie?"

Val's hands trembled. She looked to Chrissy for an answer, but the blonde was busy monitoring Monica and the immediate surrounding. The windmaker opened her mouth to speak, but couldn't form a sentence.

"Cat got your tongue, dear?"

Chrissy's veins popped. "Fuck off, Monica."

"Why so antagonistic, Miss Chrissy?" The metal fan folded her arms. "I swear, we haven't had a decent conversation in a while."

"There's nothing to talk about." Chrissy maintained her focus. "You stole our rings, and now you want to steal my employees." She squinted. "I don't know why you won't just leave us alone."

"Well that's precisely why we should have ourselves a little talk!" Monica merrily plopped herself on the rooftop. "Where should I begin?"

"I'm not interested." Val stepped forward. Chrissy looked to her briefly, then continued staring forward.

The new hire continued. "I t-think gender inequality is an important issue... I-I'm just not interested in joining your team." She looked to the gravel floor. "I'm sorry."

Monica tilted her head down and nodded. After a few moments, she smiled.

"I can't say I didn't see this coming, Valorie. As I suspected, you fear change because you, like me, fear the unknown." Bloody Mary leaned back and looked to the obscure sky above. "Nevertheless, I'm disappointed in your decision."

Electricity shot up over the edge of the building behind Val and Chrissy. Eliza zipped above in a flash and landed next to Monica with her back turned to the duo. She slowly rotated her head and winked at Val. Tongues of energy licked her all over as she stood and crossed her arms with delight.

"You can't fear change, Miss Valorie." Monica stared at Val with a smirk. "It'll help you grow even stronger."

"Leave us alone, Monica." Chrissy dug her feet into the rooftop. "Valorie gave you her answer. It's time to leave now."

"I'll depart on my own accord, thank you." The foreigner stretched her hands above her head. "I'm not under your employ anymore, love."

The blonde scoffed. A cluster of clouds parted overhead and shone light on Monica's black ring.

"Why did you do it?" Chrissy narrowed her eyes. "Why did you steal our rings? Was it just to satisfy your agenda?"

"If by 'agenda' you mean bringing about an end to inequality among men and women, then yes, absolutely." Monica shrugged. "Honestly, I fail to understand why my theft is such a big deal to you. To my knowledge, you and your team have plenty of other rings in your arsenal."

"That's not what pisses me off." Chrissy furrowed her brow. "We considered you a friend, and you stabbed us in the back."

"I see." Monica looked up at her glowing companion and smiled. "You probably won't be happy with what I'm about to do to you next, then."

She stood and twisted her back deliberately. "Miss Valorie, you should know that if you are not with us, you are against us." The shadowmancer stretched her shoulders next. "Are you certain about your decision?"

A bead of sweat rolled down Val's cheek. Her legs started to wobble. She looked to Chrissy for an answer again, but quickly realized that she still had to speak for herself.

Val pleaded. "We d-don't have to fight. We can c-co-exist." She took a deep breath and exhaled before continuing. "We can s-split the bars—"

"That's not what we want, dear."

Val took a step back. Monica adjusted her bangs and crossed her arms.

"We want the rest of your rings."

Chrissy squeezed her fists tighter. She spoke in a low voice. "Why?"

Monica chuckled. "To destroy them, of course."

The boss lady slammed her foot on the roof, causing cracks to splinter into a million directions. The headbanger and her loli hardly flinched.

"Do you know how much I've had to sacrifice?!" Chrissy's face reddened with anger. "Do you have any idea what I've had to do to protect them?!"

"I don't care, frankly." Monica kept her composure. "In order to fulfill my so-called 'agenda,' there's simply no other way."

"I don't understand." Blondie shook her head. "Why are you doing this?!"

The Conjurer placed her hands on her hips. "I think I've made it quite clear, dear!" She cleared her throat before continuing. "In this city, men consume alcohol to no end. These pigs, in turn, do unspeakable things to women in their stupor."

Monica kicked some gravel in front of her. "It's simple, really. Once we destroy the rings, the patriarchy won't be as complacent. Women won't have to hide anymore. It's the first step on our path to revolutionize society."

"We're saving people from themselves!" The veins on Chrissy's face protruded dramatically. "Men *and* women. Your cause doesn't make any sense!"

"It does, Miss Chrissy, and you know it." Monica looked to her hand. It blackened into a claw. "I envision a city where little girls won't have to be afraid of their fathers." Her nails grew sharper. "A place where women no longer fear the strange man watching from the shadows."

"M-Monica..." Val tried her best to muster more courage. "I-I think you have good in-intentions." She hesitated briefly. "Let's r-reach an agreement when t-this nightmare is—"

"No, Valorie." Monica's other hand turned to shadow. "No woman should use the rings from this point forward." The talons on her left claw sharpened. "Our revolution begins tonight."

"We'll agree to disagree." Chrissy focused her blue eyes squarely on the rocker's face. "I'm not holding back, Monica. I'll give you one last chance to leave."

The Conjurer smirked. "Before we begin, I just want to point out how proud I am of you, Miss Valorie. You've transformed into a fine woman." She shrugged. "I would've liked to see you evolve further under my tutelage, but I suppose beggars can't be choosers."

Val looked down at the rooftop, unsure of what to say. Her heart was beating fast. She was dizzy from the anxiety.

Chrissy stepped in for her. "It's time to shut the hell up, Monica."

The shadowmancer shook her head. "Piss off."

Bossy pounced. Monica ran forward, her arms opening wide and her claws expanding fast. Eliza set her sights on Val.

The puppy spread her paws out over the gravel. Itty-bitty streaks of lightning sprang from her fingertips before she ripped over 9,000 watts of electricity toward the bewildered bartender.

The airbender pushed air to her side and dodged the wave. Eliza closed the gap in a second and latched onto her prey. She pushed off, flinging both of them from the roof into the gray abyss below.

Val's heart nearly beat out of her chest. She pushed her attacker as they fell, desperately trying to concentrate wind between them.

Eliza noticed and gripped onto Val tighter. Sparks bounced off her fingertips.

"Bye-bye, crybaby."

She electrocuted the windmaker in midair.

Several weeks prior, Monica and Eliza gulped alcohol in the alleyway adjacent to the 'Three-Legged Cowboy.' After letting the booze marinate in their systems for a few minutes, the pair slipped on their rings and disappeared, leaving nothing but sack slings and ball stretchers behind them.

They appeared on a bed next to a giant naked Ken doll. One wore a ballet dress reminiscent of a black swan. The other was dressed entirely in pink, accessorized from head to toe in the latest faux bling.

Eliza smacked the mound where the boy toy's junk should've been.

"Ha, you've got no dick!"

Monica giggled. "Come now, Liza. You know as well as I that this isn't any jolly old place."

The rocker jumped off the mattress, walked across the plastic floor and glanced through the cutout window. An avenue of dollhouses lined a motionless suburban street. The air smelled like nail polish and sticky issues of male fitness magazines. Ken clones stood by lawnmowers, mailboxes and grills with creepy acrylic grins plastered on their faces.

For Monica, this was the ultimate nightmare. She gently touched her stomach wounds. Most had healed, but she was in no shape to fight yet.

The alcohol helped. She took a sip of her Bloody Mary and returned her gaze to the window.

"Fuck!"

A woman screamed down the road. An explosion suddenly rocked their fuchsia two-story mansion - complete with Malibu convertible - and tossed a myriad of choking hazards off the shelves.

"Is that Barbie?"

"Keep quiet, Liza. *Someone* is on her way."

Monica leaned against the wall to get a better look. She witnessed throwing knives slash a Ken into jewelry bracelets. A chain danced in the air before offing the heads of an entire school bus of handsome blonde beach bums. Smiling heads bounced around a familiar stoner as she blew up a pair of pecs with a ninja star.

"I see the cantankerous one has joined us this evening."

Missy wore short overalls underneath a flannel blouse. A sweaty neckerchief and high leather boots accentuated the piece. The swordbearer couldn't have cared less for fashion.

Another lasso of steel wrapped around a spray-tanned male bimbo and threw him into the sky like an unmade cheese pizza. It grabbed him midair, cooked him on a grill and turned him into lamb chops.

Missy's rampage continued a little more before Chrissy arrived on the scene.

"Having fun yet?"

The boss lady adorned a pink shawl over a silver-lined ballroom gown. A tiara sat peacefully on her radiant yellow head. Her employee shook her head.

"You're loving this, aren't you?"

Chrissy laughed. "Perks of the job!"

Missy grumbled, picked up a mailbox and impaled Dr. Ken three doors down.

Blondie crossed her arms. "Have you had something to drink yet?"

The pothead squinted. "No."

Chrissy nodded. "Drink something. You get a little homicidal when you're thirsty."

Missy sighed, dug out her Rusty Nail and took a sip. Her leader smiled.

"Better?"

"Better."

"Good." Chrissy motioned Missy to come closer. "Shall we take a walk until our monster shows up?"

The Conjurer returned the smile. "Sure."

Monica watched the pair amble down the street together. She noticed Missy link her arm around her boss. Monica pointed and whispered to Eliza.

"Ha! Gay!"

Electro scowled. "That's not very nice of you!"

The shadowmancer shrugged. "I'm just trying to lighten the mood. My apologies." They continued their observation unnoticed.

"Hey, Chris?" Missy looked down at the ground as they strolled along. "Can we talk about what happened to Vera?"

Chrissy frowned. "Miss, I…" She hesitated and looked away. "I don't know what to say."

The cowboy stopped walking. She took a deep breath and stared at her boss in the eyes.

"I think you need to fire Sissy."

Monica and Eliza raised their eyebrows.

Blondie exhaled loudly. She unlinked her arm with Missy's and sat down on the curb, her heels clipping against the hollow street. Missy sat beside her and waited before speaking again.

"I trust you with my life, Chris." The slasher folded her arms across her chest. "You know what's best for me and the team. I'm not doubting you at all." She scratched her messy hair. "I just think it's for the best, especially with Valorie now on board."

Her leader looked ahead, clearly wrestling with what to say. Missy nervously dug into her pocket and produced a cigarette and a lighter. She ignited and took a toke before Chrissy spoke again.

"Sissy is such an important part of our team." She removed the tiara off her head and watched it shine in the light. "She gets shit done as soon as I ask." The Special traced around the jewel in the middle of the band. "But I understand where you're going from. Sissy is—"

"Dangerous, Chris." Missy blew a long smoke cloud in front of her. "What happened to Vera was her fault. We both saw that."

Chrissy sunk her face into her arms. She mumbled, "I don't know, Miss. I really don't know."

"I'm worried about us, too." The chain-wielder rolled her wand between two fingers. "She could hurt you or me next…" She smut a bit of the cigarette on the curb and added in a low voice, "And I don't know what I'd do without you."

Chrissy lifted her head and looked ahead blankly. "Maybe… maybe she's had a change of heart now that she's in the hospital."

"Chris, she almost shot Val." Missy drew from her stick again. She puffed out another cloud. "I don't think we should take our chances."

Fisticuffs nodded slightly and returned to her thoughts.

Monica whispered to Eliza. "I presume Vera was another girl they sought to hire." She paused. "I suppose it didn't turn out well for her."

The menace with hair drills made a sad face. "What do you think happened?"

The shadowmancer took a deep breath. "I have no idea, but the volatile one likely had something to do with it."

The pair peeked back out their window just as Chrissy spoke up again.

"I'll protect Valorie, Miss." Boss lady gripped onto the curb. "And we'll keep a close eye on Siss from this point forward."

Missy flickered her cigarette to the opposite end of the street. "We need to train Valorie really well." She stared as tiny streams of smoke billow from her crumbled up wand. "And tell her about Siss before she comes back."

"We've got a little more time." Chrissy stood. She extended a hand to her employee. "We'll make sure that we're all safe."

Missy bobbed her head. "Alright, I trust you." She grabbed her boss' hand and stood up beside her. Before letting go, she leaned in close and spoke softly in the brawler's ear.

"But the moment she tries to hurt one of us again, I'm wrapping her up and taking off her ring."

Chrissy grinned. "Thank you, Miss. For everything."

Missy backed away. "Yeah, whatever." She smiled.

The two continued walking down the sidewalk side by side. Monica sunk away from the cutout and held her chin.

"It seems the redhead is just as homicidal as she is formidable."

"I wouldn't know. You were the one that worked for them." Eliza shrugged. "Taking her out was easy for me, but I think I caught her off-guard."

"Yes." Monica tilted her head and looked at Chrissy and Missy's backs as they sauntered away. She felt the wounds in her stomach burn. "I consider myself lucky."

Puppy nodded. The thief continued. "Nevertheless, our cause lives on." She smirked. "We'll just have to make a few more friends soon."

Grayscale began seeping into the corner of the room. Eliza clapped. "Oh, looks like the show is starting!"

Monica looked out the window. Monochrome began blotting haphazard areas around the neighborhood.

"The future looks bright for us, dear."

***

As she collapsed from a cloud of ash, Val could make out the street fast approaching. She swung a gust of wind to the ground with the last bit of consciousness left in her system, cushioning her landing and helping her rest gently on her face.

She moved her lightly charred hand over to her pocket, feeling the tin of alcohol she kept there. Eliza arrived seconds after Val, tossing a shockwave to land neatly on two feet. She smiled at her adversary as the dust mingled with sparks of electricity.

Lizard noticed Val removing the alcohol from her pocket. She chuckled.

"Guzzle it down, crybaby!" She put her hands on her hips. "You're gonna need it!"

Val twisted the cap slowly, her hands barely moving due to the exhaustion. She put the tin to her lips and inhaled her Orgasm, desperately hoping it would redeem her.

She returned the bottle to her pocket after drinking and waited on the ground for the juice to kick in. Eliza tapped her foot.

"I don't have all day, you know."

Val breathed in, breathed out. She pictured her mother telling her to stand up. She told herself to face her fears.

The airbender scratched the floor, then shifted her entire body weight onto her palms. She lifted her torso and, one by one, slipped both her legs underneath her. She stood up feebly, wishing she was the one who took the day off today.

Val looked tiredly at the glowing underage chick a few meters away. She wondered how the hell she was going to get out of this alive.

"Good job, wimpy kid!" Eliza giggled. "Now give me your ring, pwease."

The new hire shook her frail head. She barely spoke above a whisper, but she made her message clear.

"No."

Eliza tilted her head, unsure if Val was being confident or stupid. She shrugged. "Have it your way, I guess."

The electrocutioner stretched her quadriceps. Val watched, still struggling to find a way out.

"Hey, did your boss ever tell you about Vera?"

The windmaker squinted at Eliza, annoyed, fatigued and confused.

"No."

"That's interesting!" The toddler stretched her arms next. "You know, me and Monica are actually helping you in a way." She rotated her neck around in a circle. "If we didn't take your rings, your coworker would've killed you!"

Val failed to make the connection at that moment. She was busy thinking of a way to escape.

"Yup, that Sissy is trouble!" Eliza leaned back, cracking her latissimus dorsi and lower spine. "We've gotta watch out for that one!"

She dipped forward and touched her toes. Breezy seized her chance.

Val summoned the last traces of energy inside her, opened her eyes wide and reached a palm overhead. She waved it fast in front of her, causing a sharp surge of air to drop on Liza's back.

The tiny one squealed as the top of her head slammed into the concrete. A dust cloud puffed up, temporarily obscuring her line of vision. Val sunk her right foot back and breathed in, breathed out. She hoped the adrenaline would help steer her straight.

"Ragh!"

The bender kicked off. A strong airstream rolled in behind her. She soared through the dust cloud and pointed her arms forward like Superman. She told herself not to look back once she passed the first intersection.

Eliza spun around with unraveled ponytails. She pointed her index finger at the maid flying away from her. Electricity burned through her sleeve and bounced off her arm.

"Nice try, loser."

A lightning bolt exploded from her digit.

Even while looking ahead, Val saw light flash in front of her. A boom came next, deafening her right ear. She panicked and shifted her weight leftward, hoping to smoothly turn around the next intersection.

The airstream grew weak. Her foot poked the ground. Val tried to lift herself with wind. Her juice had run out.

She skidded on the road and rolled a handful of times before coming to a full stop. The entire right side of her body ached. She could taste blood oozing from her nostrils.

Val looked up to the sky and desperately tried to breathe. The air failed to ease her nerves.

She could faintly hear her heartbeat pulse. Playful skips caught up to her.

Eliza entered Val's field of vision. "Sorry that I missed." She crouched over the Emitter's head. "This'll be a lot less painful."

The electrocutioner pressed an illuminated index finger on Val's forehead. The new hire went unconscious immediately, her open eyes still staring at the gray clouds above.

***

In a faraway place, a television monitor buzzed to life.

"Christine really liked watching TV!" A narrator spoke behind the letters H-D-M-I. "It was her best friend."

A static image of a young Chrissy sitting in front of a screen appeared. The overenthusiastic voice continued.

"Mommy never really wanted to play, but that's OK. Christine could play by herself in front of the TV!"

The slideshow continued with an image of the blonde in a school uniform. "Christine had to walk home from school by herself every day." It transitioned to a close-up of a smile on Chrissy's face. "But when she returned, there were lots of great cartoons on TV!"

An image of a yellow-haired celebrity popped up. "TV taught her everything about growing up. She learned that she could be anything she wanted if she was pretty and boys liked her!"

Hair dye dotted the edges of a sink next. "Christine changed herself so she could look like the girls on TV. She stole lots of Mommy's money and went to the salon every week!"

The monitor blackened. Equidistant gray bars floated up. The narrator spoke in a softer tone. "Mommy didn't like Christine stealing her money, so she hit her sometimes." The voice perked up quickly. "But at least she looked like the girls on TV!"

A picture of high school-aged Chrissy appeared. She stood motionlessly in the center with a blank expression on her face.

"Mommy started hitting Christine more and more. Christine didn't want the boys at school to notice!"

The last shot showed Chrissy walking down a suburban street with a television in her arms.

The voice happily exclaimed, "Christine ran away from home with her best friend, the TV!"

***

A lonely composite cable frolicked in the nighttime breeze.

Val regained her senses on the gravel rooftop from earlier. Her hearing had nearly restored itself, but the entire right side of her body still throbbed. She wondered what she had permanently broken.

The sky was pitch black. Something illuminated her from behind. She rotated her head nervously.

A giant businessman dressed in gray and white stripes stared down at the rooftop. Its 72-foot flat screen head flickered static while its white alabaster hands clutched onto the railing.

A familiar blonde's body lay unmoving in the light. It took a few seconds for Val to realize who it was.

"Chrissy!"

Val shifted weight to her upper body and pushed off the ground. She stood up slowly, being careful to rely only on her left side. She took a step forward. It hurt like hell.

"Chrissy, can you hear me?!"

Her employer wasn't responding. The businessman continued looking down, still and emotionless. Val told herself she needed to move closer.

After several excruciating steps, the TV head tilted its head slightly. The light from its screen shone directly into Val's eyes and temporarily blinded her. It glared at her for a minute before returning to Chrissy.

The monster's right hand let go of the rooftop's railing. It lifted high into the sky, palm wide open. The monitor continued beaming below. Val breathed heavy.

"Chrissy, wake the hell up!"

The windmaker moved forward briskly, wincing every time her right foot touched the ground. Chrissy was still unconscious.

The entrepreneur's hand had reached its apex. Val hobbled as fast as she could. Tears streamed down her face.

Her voice cracked. "Chrissy!"

The alabaster hand slammed onto the sleeping blonde. Gore sheeted its face all the way across.

Val ragdolled across the rooftop with uniform dripping dark red. She banged her head hard on the opposite railing and fell face-first onto the tiny rocks below.

She couldn't feel her body anymore. It was if it instantly knew everything had changed.

Permanently scarred, Val dared herself to get up one last time. She shifted her weight to her torso again. The light from the colossus shone on *her* now.

As she stood, she told herself not to think of her boss. She wouldn't survive if she allowed her mind to wander.

Water poured down Val's face as she formed a fist. She squinted up at the floating behemoth. Its bloodied alabaster hand opened wide to catch her.

She screamed and let a fist fly in front of her. A gust of wind cracked the flat screen and sent shards of glass flying.

It wasn't enough. Wide-eyed, Val fumbled through her pockets. Her alcohol was gone.

"I'd hate to see you go so soon, Miss Valorie."

Monica's formless voice sounded like nails on a chalkboard for Val. The new hire blamed herself for everything.

The titan continued unfazed. It opened its hand and reached for its next victim.

"You won't die today."

The light from the monitor vanished. The businessman froze in the dark.

"I want you to see what happens next on our journey."

Sparks jumped from the back of the screen. Someone was cutting the wires that gave it life.

"I want you to realize the consequences of your mistakes."

A great light flashed from the spine of the creature.

"See you next time, dear."

The show had come to an end for good.

***

Val stumbled into her apartment hours after her shift was over. The broken pieces of a yellow ring jumped around in her pocket.

Missy slouched on her torn-up sofa, messing around with the television remote.

"Everyone make it back in one piece, fuckwad?"

Chapter 8
Soggy Biscuit

Silvia found herself passing out fliers to pus-filled otaku on the grundle between Anusville and Scrotumberg again. Her bright red sailor uniform took in all the lights, laughter and labia that gave her city the life it desperately wanted.

She grudgingly advertised the schoolgirl-themed café she worked in, a cringe-worthy place called the Sassy Gal. At least she wasn't chatting with a 50-year-old pervert about her college class on phimosis that day.

It was getting close to midnight, which meant the town's hikikomori were about to emerge from their holes. The joshi kosei tossed up whatever she had left and made a break for it.

Silvia walked to her gonorrhea-invested train station, swiped her overpriced transit card at the gate and waited on an open-air platform.

She sat on a bench and thought about why her life was so unfair. A pasty old man shuffled his feet on the platform across from her, adorning socks beneath his sandals.

Between work and school, work and school, work and school, the part-timer didn't feel like herself anymore. She felt like a cog, turning, turning, turning to satisfy a set of infinite rules.

Her long auburn ponytail swayed lightly in the nighttime wind. Maybe she needed medication. Or maybe she was thinking too much.

A train was about to rush in front of her. The man on the other platform threw himself onto the tracks.

***

Dead crickets leaked from a tarantula's mouth inside Silvia's terrarium.

She scrolled through social media underneath her bedsheets. A message from her ex said he really wanted to be there with her.

The alarm rang. Silvia rolled out of bed and threw on the unwashed clothes that lay strewn around her room. She lurched down the stairs of her parents' house without an ounce of sleep. She skipped breakfast because she had no appetite. The front door slammed shut behind her.

Walking, walking, walking to the station. Waiting, waiting, waiting for the train. Arriving at school and learning, learning, learning about nothing.

The machine kept creeping along when she entered the Sassy Gal later that day.

She traded her oversized sweater and ripped jeans for her sailor uniform, then opened the door to the dining room. Her first customer hunched over a small pink table, patiently waiting for his favorite schoolgirl to arrive.

Silvia sat down on the cushioned seat opposite him. She smelled his cheap aftershave and tried hard not to vomit.

The man removed some loose hair from his face and flashed a wicked smile. "Hey."

"Hello."

"How are you, Silvy?"

His carcinogenic breath made Silvia's spine shiver in disgust. She kept her composure.

"Fine."

Her visitor raised an eyebrow and smirked. "Really?"

"I'm just fine."

The man looked her in the eyes. "What else?"

Silvia squinted. "Fine means fine."

Her patron leaned back. "And fine you are." His smirk made her want to stab him. "Give me a little more."

The maid pushed her chair away and stood up. "I'll make us coffee." She was seconds away from both regurgitating and committing murder. She couldn't decide which she wanted to do first.

Silvia walked over to the Sassy Gal's food and beverage station. She grabbed two mugs and flipped them over, then poured coffee from an urn. The liquid that flowed out reflected her likeness in black.

She returned to the tiny table and placed two mugs between herself and her customer.

The man scratched his untrimmed sideburns. "Why don't you ever want to talk to me?" He leaned in close and clasped his dirty hands around the mug. "I pay good money to see you every week." The crusts of his overgrown fingernails were brown. His putrid breath suffocated the joshi kosei's nostrils.

Silvia retreated slightly in her seat, making sure to keep a cool head. She took a sip of her coffee and spoke softly.

"Because I fucking hate you."

The man laughed out loud. "There we are!" He nodded his head approvingly. "There's my little Silvy."

Silvia drank from her mug again. She tapped her toes beneath the table, hoping it'll help ease her desire to douse her visitor's face in hot liquid.

"Listen to me, Silvy." The man shifted his chair closer, spilling some of his coffee onto the table. "How about I pick you up outside when your shift is over?" He grinned. "We both know you haven't had a good fuck in a while."

The redhead looked into her mug. "Go to hell."

The man leaned back again. He lifted his mug with a filthy hand and raised it to his girl.

"Never change Silvy." He drank with a smile. "Never change."

✳✳✳

Maggots festered in a cat's underbelly on the road near an apartment complex.

Silvia scrolled through social media underneath her ex-boyfriend's sheets. She told him the night before that this would be the last time. They both knew she was lying.

She climbed out of bed quietly, put her clothes on and tiptoed out the door. She walked, walked, walked to the station, waited, waited, waited for the train. She traveled to school and learned, learned, learned about nothing.

The cog kept turning when she showed up to work that night. She put on her uniform and opened the door to the dining room. The man from yesterday was waiting for her at their favorite table.

She sat down across from him again, holding her breath lest she smell his cheap aftershave. The man leaned forward and cut to the chase.

"I've been feeling really horny today, Silvy." He looked around to see if anyone was watching, then reached down to his crotch and adjusted his member. "I'll make you a deal. Come to my place tonight and I'll give you $300 tomorrow morning. You won't even have to blow me."

Silvia folded her hands on the table and looked directly at the man in front of her. His light brown eyes were red around the edges, his teeth were yellow with built-up plaque and his sideburns had begun to invade the rest of his face. She couldn't feel sorry for him even if she tried.

The schoolgirl cleared her throat. "No, you piece of shit."

The man sighed, leaned away and slicked his greasy hair back. He glanced at another table and noticed one of her colleagues chatting happily to a guest. He pointed with his chin.

"Why don't you show me the same respect, Silvy. I pay a lot of money to see every night."

Silvia looked down at her hands and nodded. "I'll get you a cookie."

She stood up and walked over to the food and beverage station. She grabbed a small dish, opened up a jar and picked up a chocolate chip cookie with tongs. She returned to her customer, placing the cookie between them.

The unsatisfied man broke apart a piece of dessert with one hand. He ate it with his rancid mouth wide open, crumbs sprinkling the table Silvia had to clean once he left.

Her patron smiled. "I love you, Silvy."

The joshi kosei stared past the man with a blank expression, trying hard not to feel anything at all.

***

A stray dog licked itself behind a fast-food restaurant.

Silvia walked, walked, walked to the station, waited, waited, waited for the train. She traveled to school and learned, learned, learned about nothing.

The engine rumbled on when she showed up to the Sassy Gal that evening.

Once again, she traded her usual hastily put together getup for the schoolgirl outfit. She stepped out to the dining room to entertain her number one fan.

She sat down across from the man. He already had a grin plastered on his face. She folded her hands on the small table and waited for him to begin talking.

The man leaned forward and whispered merrily. "I fucked a whore yesterday, Silvy."

Silvia looked at him stoically. She spoke softly. "Congratulations."

Her customer scratched his face and bared his yellow teeth. "Do you want to know the best part?"

The redhead shook her head and tilted her eyes down. She already knew the answer. "No, I don't."

The man giggled. "I imagined I was fucking you instead."

Silvia nodded. She closed her eyes for a few seconds and allowed the rage inside her to subside. She calmly asked, "What can I get for you tonight, sir?"

Her guest wiped his nose with a finger and licked his lips. "I still want you, Silvy. Really badly."

He reached down to his crotch again. He got up momentarily to shift his boner, then chuckled when he sat back down.

"What can I say?" He slicked his hair back and leaned in once more. "You're the only one for me."

Silvia could feel her head grow numb from the blood pressure. She moved her hands underneath the table when they began vibrating in anger.

The man stared at her in silence, admiring the view from the comfort of his chair. Silvia pulled back and said, "I need to use the ladies' room. Excuse me."

As she walked away, she could feel his eyes glued to her ass.

She grabbed the key to the restroom from the food and beverage station and walked out of the café to a narrow stairwell. She climbed up a flight and inserted the key into a door, then twisted and opened her way to the dark ladies' room.

She turned on the lights and looked into a sink. She spun the faucet handles furiously and screamed as loud as she could.

✳✳✳

Silvia stared up at the ceiling in her bedroom. She couldn't help but feel she was walking, walking, walking in circles, waiting, waiting, waiting for fate. Getting nowhere. Learning, learning, learning about nothing.

She turned to her side and closed her eyes. Her temple pulsed at the thought of her shift that night and how powerless she was to do anything about it.

She rotated over to the opposite side of her bed. She could change her gig, but concluded a long time ago that she'd be treated the same everywhere.

Silvia's mind was quickly overwhelmed by increasingly negative thoughts. She needed to breathe. She gently stepped out from underneath the covers, tiptoed down the stairs of her parents' house and opened the front door silently.

She ambled down a suburban sidewalk with nothing but the silence of night to ease her anxiety. As she approached the curb, she looked up to the sky and tried counting the stars she saw there.

She couldn't find any.

The joshi kosei arrived at an intersection and wondered which direction she should veer off to. A familiar man behind her offered a suggestion.

"I'm right here, Silvy."

Silvia spun around in surprise. Her repeat customer stood so close he assaulted her nostrils with cheap aftershave. She backed away to the edge of the curb, squinted her eyes and looked her stalker in the face with visible resentment.

"What the fuck are you doing here?"

The man giggled. "I know how lonely you've been." He licked his lips and slicked back his hair. "My car is down the block. You ready?"

"You fucking followed me." Silvia stepped away into the street, ready to run in a moment's notice. "You're a fucking lunatic."

"I'm not much, Silvy." He grinned. "Just a man who needs a good fuck."

The redhead's heart was beating fast. She tried mapping out an escape plan in her mind.

"Come on." The man extended his filthy arm. "Let's make love tonight."

Silvia clenched her fists and bared her teeth. "Go to hell."

She jumped back, spun around and ran fast down the middle of the street, hoping that a car would be headed her way. She didn't see headlights. She had no other choice.

"Help!"

The man pinned her down hard, landing her face-first into the concrete. Her vision bounced in a dozen different directions. Saliva oozed from the man's mouth onto Silvia's hair.

The excited patron placed one hand behind his prey's head and pushed down hard, forcing her to cough and inhale dirt. He rested his elbow on her back to stop her squirming, then slipped his other hand beneath the hem of her pajama pants.

He laughed loudly and spilled more of his spit onto Silvia. He pulled back her pants and exposed her naked ass to the night. He squeezed a cheek with his brown fingernails and leaned down toward Silvia's face.

"Don't make this hard, Silvy."

He removed his hand off her head and sat on top of her. He cupped a hand over her mouth before she could scream again.

His other hand crept up her torso and stopped at her left breast. He squeezed it and laughed excitedly into Silvia's ear.

Silvia had given up on her life. She wanted to be saved from the monotony of her commute, her work, her school. This was the universe's answer. This is what she deserved.

A beer bottle smashed over her assailant's head, rendering him immediately unconscious.

He collapsed to the street with a thud, his face lined with scratches. The redhead rotated her head and saw the man's disgusting mouth drool uncontrollably on the ground. She thought he looked dead. She couldn't understand what was happening.

She stood, pulled her pants up and turned around, tears streamed down her cheeks. She stared at the pair that saved her.

One wore long black bangs over her right eye and jeans torn in strange places. The other wore yellow hair drills and held a brown paper bag in her hand.

Silvia opened her quivering mouth to say something. She couldn't place her words in a sentence. The anger, desperation, self-loathing, anxiety, sadness had reached an apex.

She sank to her knees and cried. She cried, cried, cried.

Monica and Eliza stood above her. They looked at each other and smiled.

The shadowmancer tossed the broken bottle in her hand over her shoulder and crouched down next to Silvia. She placed a hand on her back.

"How about we buy you a drink tomorrow night, love?"

Not long after that, Silvia's life changed forever.

***

The schoolgirl woke up in a bright white room the day after. She rubbed her eyes beneath a thick comforter on a large canopy bed. It didn't take her long to notice the red ring on her index finger.

She stared at her new jewelry and wondered how it managed to get there. She lifted the blanket and discovered she was wearing her sailor uniform.

The sight of her work getup helped her remember the 24 hours that led her to where she was. The sirens of police cars and the man's miserable pleas. Washing her hair repeatedly while sobbing in the shower. Sleeping in for most of the afternoon.

Responding to her ex's sex request by telling him to kill himself. Not showing up to work. Tossing her uniform in the garbage can outside before meeting two chicks for drinks.

She remembered the conversation she had with the rocker girl, Monica. The foreigner asked if she was tired of being treated like an animal by men. Silvia said she wished she could do something about it.

She may have had too many Fiery Apples that night. She looked around the room and noted how barren it was. Nothing but a vanity set and computer desk occupied the space. The door was hidden somewhere.

Silvia tossed the sheets and scooted to the edge of the mattress. She stood, bent over and inspected the floor underneath her bed. She didn't find anything there.

The redhead got up and walked to the vanity set next, her heart beating faster with every step. She swiveled it slightly out of place and looked behind. No door there.

It must be behind the computer desk, she thought. She strode over to the work area and pulled it forward. She only found a handful of cables.

The joshi kosei sat down on the white swivel chair in front of the desk, scanning every corner of the room for signs of a latch or cord. Someone started speaking to her.

"Hi Silvy."

Silvia turned around to see the face of her stalker float on the computer monitor in front of her. A tiny light by the webcam camera shone straight into her eyes.

She jolted around the desk and unplugged the cables. The man laughed through the screen's built-in speakers.

"Nice try." He smiled wide. "That's not how this works."

Wide-eyed, she raced back around and covered the webcam with her hand, then pressed on the ESC key. It didn't work. She noticed the man slick back his hair while grinning ear to ear.

CTRL, ALT, DELETE were next. Nothing. She swung around the mouse. No cursor.

The man giggled incessantly. Silvia felt the monitor's volume rise. Blood rushed to her head.

In a fit of rage and desperation, she ripped the screen from its perch, shrieked and slammed it down hard on the bedroom floor. Glass slipped across the white surface. The man's face froze in place. His laughing stopped.

As adrenaline coursed through Silvia's veins, the waistband of her skirt loosened on its own. She caught it before it fell to the ground. In response, the article of clothing ripped to shreds from the hem up.

The man's laughing continued on cue. The bottom edge of her blouse was next. As tiny pieces sprinkled onto the floor, the man happily exclaimed, "You'll never escape it, Silvy!" It was as if he was speaking through a boombox now. "I'll always be with you!"

Just as her blouse had torn itself apart, the elastic around her underwear had loosened.

Silvia had had enough. She was tired of playing the schoolgirl, the victim, the fantasy.

The room roared with the redhead as a vortex of fire burned around her. The bed sunk into itself, the vanity set crumbled and turned to ash, and the monitor faded into oblivion.

She screamed for her life. The whiteness of the room was gone. It had all been charred to black.

Embers tiptoed and danced in circles. As the flames subsided, Silvia's lips curled into a smile. The strangeness of gray dipped into black.

***

The pyromancer opened her eyes on the counter of a bar, her drink spilled and her hair wet. She tilted her head up and glanced back down on the red ring around her finger. She pulled it off and rested it in the palm of her hand silently.

"Hell of a night, dear."

Monica stood behind her. Silvia noticed that she too wore a ring, albeit black. Her hand was clasped around a nearly empty glass of Bloody Mary.

The shadowmancer set her drink on the counter and leaned in close to the redhead's ear. "How about a career change?"

Monica stepped back and smiled. Silvia noticed the other girl, Eliza, waiting by the exit.

"I'll be waiting, Silvia." The rocker walked away to the door and slipped out with her partner.

The joshi kosei looked back down at the ring in her hand.

Chapter 9
Dickbutt

A lonely cricket chirped on a long stalk of grass by the waterfront. A lonely girl counted the stars in the sky above.

"W-Who's Vera?"

"What? What are you talking—"

"W-Who is she?"

"What's going on? Where's Chris?"

Val sat up and looked behind her. Guests were seating themselves on the patio. The ceremony was about to begin.

"You're a fucking liar."

"I-I'm not… I'm so sorry Missy. I'm so so sorry."

"You fucking liar!"

She sat in the back row, feeling out of place with her mid-length black dress. The rest of the audience didn't care. None of this was real anyway.

"Is S-Sissy dangerous?"

"What the fuck are you saying?"

"I don't want to die."

"You just let Chris die!"

"That wasn't my goddamn fault!"

The moon illuminated the dark blue backdrop on the altar and cast shadows on the anxious face of a groom. Cold numbed Val's fingertips when the bride finally made her way down the aisle.

"You fucking murdered my best friend! You killed her!"

"Missy, stop! Where the hell are you going?!"

"I need… to leave."

"We need to stick together."

"Fuck you!"

A replica of the pixie-cut beauty walked down the aisle on her own. No one but Val turned their head.

"You killed her. You fucking killed Chrissy."

The bride stood on the stage and stared into her groom's eyes. The priest smiled as he spoke. The temperature plummeted fast. Val leaned back in her chair.

"Do you take this woman to be your wedded wife?"

"I do."

"Do you take this man to be your wedded husband?

"I do."

Val closed her eyes and remembered the last words Missy spoke to her.

"I'll never fucking forgive you."

The priest slammed his bible and proclaimed, "I hereby pronounce you husband and wife!"

A lonely tear rolled down Val's check. The holy man bellowed.

"You may now kiss the bride!"

The groom opened his mouth wide and leaned his head back. Long, canine-like incisors spouted from his lips. He sprung forward and dug his maw into his bride's neck.

Val had only caught a glimpse of the attack before the audience rose in cheer. She moved her seat back and ran to the aisle. The monster had already devoured the top half of his bride's corpse.

A bloodied skull rolled down the steps of the altar as red oozed out to the congregation. Val stood in place wide-eyed, unsure of what she should do next.

Her hand formed a fist on its own. She breathed in, breathed out and ripped a surge of air forward.

The groom and his meal were directly hit by the blast. A dust cloud billowed forward as the wedding's guests continued their incessant raving.

Val watched the cloud subside, her fists ready to launch more blows if needed. A gray door materialized where the beast and his victim used to be. Everyone on the altar had disappeared.

The airbender walked down the aisle as the crowd continued its clapping and cheering. They played their parts, in spite of the interruption. She tried not to notice the splashing of her steps or the blood seeping into her ballerina shoes.

She climbed up to the door, placed her hand on the knob and told herself that she'd be OK no matter what she found on the other side. Val turned the knob and entered.

The whooping of the audience had instantly ceased the moment she gently closed the door behind her. Rows of shelves were illuminated only by a singular ceiling panel in the distance. The racks collected dozens of jars, each filled with clear liquid and indistinguishable black globs.

Val kept her fists clenched as she stepped forward with uncertainty. Her footfall echoed in the chamber, reminding her she was alone. These days, only her thoughts kept her company.

It had been a month since her former roommate packed up her things and left the apartment. The Conjurer never showed up to work, leaving Val to fend for herself. The newbie had so far managed on her own, but she had no idea what would happen when Sissy showed up soon.

She didn't care about what happened to Vera anymore. She just wanted her foul-mouthed stoner back.

As Val walked closer to the light, she tried examining the jars more carefully. The pinkish hue of the subjects inside them reminded her of a naked mole-rat at first. When the organisms rotated, she noticed tiny human-like arms and legs.

Val's eyes opened wide the instant she realized what she was staring at. She backed away fast, nearly crashing into the opposite row.

As if offended by Val's reaction, the jar vibrated to the edge of its bracket, tilted and crashed dramatically on the floor. The windmaker could feel its liquid splash on her face.

A jar above tipped and spilled on Val's arm. She could feel a fragile set of lifeless fingers brush her skin.

The nightmare novice made a run for it. More glass tilted, spilled and crashed onto the floor. Tiny umbilical cords wrung around knots in her hair. Embryos slipped through her dress.

Val passed through dust motes circling beneath the light panel and continued sprinting in the dark. She shielded her face from the jars shattering in front of her. Her black gown was soaked by a mixture of formaldehyde, glutaraldehyde and methanol.

The airbender nearly broke her nose on the exit door. She clawed the egress blindly, hoping that a jar wouldn't smash on her head. After a few seconds of searching, she finally found a knob.

She turned it and fell through to the other side. She panted as a chill breeze blew through the steel-ringed fence in the alleyway she found herself in. Val couldn't begin to imagine the pain her former roommate had gone through.

She closed her eyes and breathed in, breathed out. Clouds littered the sky overhead.

It was time to end this misery and kill the sword slinger's demons.

Val turned around and spotted the groom tearing apart a rib cage by a mess of trash cans. She formed a fist and pulled her arm back. Something crashed on the ground behind her.

Before she could react, a lick of flame struck the back of her right knee. Val directed the wind downward and lightly lifted herself in the air. She spun around, landed on her left foot and examined her fellow Emitter.

The redhead in blue jeans and a hoodie inhaled deeply. After holding her breath momentarily, she leaned back and exhaled a tall column of fire into the air. The flames flew down and curled around the girl when she stopped, continuously spiraling in a vortex.

Val opened her mouth wide. She didn't stand a chance on her own.

***

Earlier that day, the chalkboard sign outside a coffee shop had a drawing of dickbutt etched onto it. The sun shone happily, kindly warming everything it looked down upon.

Silvia folded her hands over a small table inside her neighborhood coffee shop. The cup of black in front of her softly emanated wisps of smoke into the air.

Monica leaned back in her chair opposite the redhead, holding a cup of warm tea and admiring the nice weather through a window. She took a sip, smiled and shifted her chair closer to the table.

"How are you today, dear?"

The former joshi kosei looked to the front door and examined the tattooed hipsters arriving and departing.

"I'm fine. How are you?"

The rocker chick clasped her cup between her hands. "Excellent, thank you. Frankly, I've been in good spirits for a while."

Silvia nodded, took a sip and asked, "Why is that?"

Monica beamed. "Well, I've been so pleased with how much our team has grown this past month. You in particular have evolved exponentially in such a short amount of time." She shook her head and looked out the window again. "Our revolution will begin sooner than we all think."

The flamethrower looked into her black pool of liquid as she spoke. "Is that why you wanted to see me before training tonight?"

"Right! Of course. We're both busy people here. I wanted to let you know in person that your training later will be a bit unexpected."

Silvia raised an eyebrow. "Isn't it always that way?"

Monica grinned. "You're right. What I mean to say is that you won't be hunting a nightmare. Rather, you'll be looking for a human being much like yourself."

The redhead squinted her eyes. This wasn't what she signed up for. "I'm hunting another magical girl?"

"I know how strange this may sound." Monica took a sip before continuing her explanation. "But this would significantly improve our efforts. I'm not asking you to injure the woman in any way. You simply need to *intimidate* her."

Silvia shook her head and leaned back with a confused expression.

"Why do you want *me* doing this?" She crossed her arms. "I'm not your hitman, Monica."

"Of course not, dear." Monica teased her bangs and looked Silvia in the eyes. "I'm simply asking that you show off what you've learned to our rival. To be perfectly honest, I ultimately desire to recruit this girl. I figured this might be a great way to evidence what she's missing."

Silvia scoffed. "So I'm your show dog, then?"

"I wouldn't think about it that way." The foreigner looked up into the air in thought. "Think of it as a roundabout means of making a new friend."

"I see." Silvia sunk her face in her cup, skeptical of Monica's intentions. She sat her coffee back down on the table and tapped her index finger nervously.

"Tell me if I'm missing something here. You want me to go into this nightmare alone, track down this girl and scare the living shit out of her, right?"

"Precisely. Eliza will be joining you. I won't be there, as I'll be scouting for more team members tonight." She sighed. "We'll have to deal with a powerful and erratic magical girl soon, and I suspect taking her down won't be as easy as the first time we faced her."

"Right." Silvia wondered if her boss and Eliza gave a damn about her. Did she just so happen to be in the right place at the right time? An image of her stalker's face flashed in her mind.

The retired schoolgirl drank the rest of her coffee and nodded. "I'll do this for you tonight, Monica." She looked in her trainer's eyes with a serious expression. "But I want your guarantee that everyone makes it back in one piece. Including the girl."

Monica sipped her tea and smirked. "You have my word."

***

Val's first instinct was to escape. She clenched a fist and punched it toward the ground, washing the pyromancer in a tidal wave of wind, extinguishing the vortex and rocketing herself high above the alleyway. She made a note of the groom's position and kicked off at her apex. Just as her leg extended back, something caught it in midair.

The airbender zoomed back down fast. The loop around her ankle started to burn. She pushed air into the alleyway just before she crashed, significantly cushioning her blow.

The new hire fell onto her side and looked back at her assailant. The hooded girl held a smoking, igneous chain around her right arm. It twisted to Val's ankle and increased its intensity.

"Ragh!"

Val could feel the molten rock burn through her skin. She reached into her dress, produced her Orgasm and downed a few gulps. It was going to be a rough night.

"Nice job, newbie!"

Eliza walked into Val's field of vision from behind. She stooped over her a few feet away. "Looks like our crybaby already wet herself!"

Silvia scoffed and yelled to her opponent. "I've got a message from my boss." She loosened the cord of lava around Val's leg and pulled it back. It crumbled to pieces right after she caught it. "She wants you to join our team."

Val winced as she stood up slowly. Eliza walked back to her colleague with a smile on her face. The windwalker breathed in, breathed out and stared at the pair in front of her.

"You can tell Monica to go fuck herself."

Val clapped her hands toward her opponents and unleashed a mini-tornado. The tempest ripped the aluminum fence from its foundation and swept the pyromaniac off her feet, tossing her into the sky and slamming her back down on the pavement hard.

Eliza evaded the onslaught by flashing above the current. She extended an arm forward and set a dozen sparks zipping Val's way. Most sunk into the airbender's skin, causing her to fall back and writhe in pain.

Electro landed by her victim and pointed her finger at Val's face. Silvia pushed her torso off the ground and realized what her partner was doing.

"Liza! Don't hurt her!" She stood up shakily, her vision still recovering from the seismic toss. "We've done enough!"

Eliza chuckled as she watched a small cloud rise from Val's body. "This is the fun part, noob! Just sit back and relax."

"No!" Silvia whipped another chain of molten rock from her arm. "Monica promised me that all we'd do is intimidate her. This is going too far!"

The loli with hair drills looked back, her finger still aimed at Val below. She put her arm on her waist, shook her head and smirked. "Don't talk back to me, *Silvy*."

The chain of fire sprang forward fast, linking around Eliza's elbow and pulling her back. The electromancer slammed her feet on the ground before she ricocheted to Silvia.

Monica's team engaged in a tug-of-war. An enraged Silvia pulled with her right arm while a ball of fire cooked in her left. Eliza pulled back despite the searing pain around her arm. Sparks of electricity danced around her body as she yelled.

"Are you sure you want to do this, *Silvy*?"

"Don't call me that, you piece of shit!"

"We saved you, idiot! You owe us!"

"I don't owe you shit!" The heat of Silvia's chain intensified. Eliza winced. "You can keep your fucking crusade!"

The redhead pulled her colleague closer. She was winning.

"I'm done with this!"

A shotgun blast disintegrated Silvia's chain in an instant. The two girls staggered backward, completely surprised by who had just arrived on the scene.

"Hello you wonderful cunts!"

Shots bounced around the ground near Eliza and Silvia's feet. An eyepatched Sissy somersaulted fast toward the loli and roundhouse kicked her in the face, knocking her unconscious immediately.

Val tilted her head up in time to witness Sissy aim a pistol at a bewildered Silvia. She remembered what Eliza told her.

The gunslinger was going to murder her.

The airbender placed the palms of her hand on the ground and pushed herself to her feet with wind. Her entire body ached as she aimed a fist back slowly. She yelled at Patchy.

"Long time no see, Sissy."

As the maniac turned around, a jetstream planted itself directly into her face, propelling her backward.

Silvia shook her head and seized her opportunity. She swung a fist into the back of Sissy's skull, knocking the lights out of her instantly.

Sissy's body hit the ground with a thud. In a matter of seconds, wind and fire stood triumphant, albeit barely.

They could hear each other pant loudly. Neither was willing to put up with that dreamscape much longer.

Val looked down on the pistol at Sissy's side. Silvia noticed her stare and walked forward. She pried the weapon from the other redhead's fingers and slid it across the pavement to the airbender.

As the weapon touched Val's feet, the pyromancer pointed to the monster still festering by the trash cans. Her fellow Emitter nodded, picked up the pistol and turned around.

The groom licked the bone of his bride's leg. Val aimed the gun directly at his face, hoping to end this nightmare and eradicate her friend's demons once and for all.

She closed her eyes, placed an index finger on the trigger, breathed in, breathed out and stared directly at her target. After a few seconds, the pistol began shaking. Val remembered the last time she held a gun. She imagined her mother's face in front of her.

Something flashed behind her. Silvia's body flung back as Sissy stood up with a laser rifle in her hands.

Before Val could react, a proton beam buzzed into her chest, right below her right shoulder.

She fell backward onto the ground. The pistol flew out of her grasp. Her entire body was paralyzed.

Sissy hummed as she passed by. "Thanks for the vidya, buddy!"

She continued forward, patting the monster on the back before turning around the corner of the alleyway.

Val witnessed the groom leisurely finish his meal. She wanted to yell for Missy to come save herself. She knew she wouldn't.

After the monster licked its lips, it leaned its head back. Its long teeth retreated into its mouth. The man resembled a normal human being again.

He walked to the end of the alleyway, looked back at Val and smiled. As a crowd of people walked by, he dug into his pocket, slipped on a pair of shades and disappeared forever.

***

When Marissa woke up in her nightmare, she found herself laying on the bed inside her first apartment. A half dozen antique swords lined the wall, just as she remembered. As she sat up, she noticed a pile of letters scattered on top of her. She picked up the first envelope and noticed it was from the clinic.

Her heart sank. She knew what memory this was. She tossed the blankets off her body and ran to her living room. Her husband was already there, sitting in his loveseat.

The man held up a glass of whiskey to their chandelier fan and tried to find the light inside it. He looked over to his wife and spoke softly.

"Come here."

Marissa walked over and stood a few feet away from the loveseat. She knew what was coming. She wanted to run out the door.

Her husband placed his glass on a small table beside his seat. A letter from a physician accompanied it. Marissa stared wide-eyed at the floor, hoping this wouldn't happen the same way.

"I read the letter."

Marissa closed her eyes, trying to prevent herself from crying. Her husband shifted in his seat and cleared his throat.

"I said I read the letter."

His wife opened her mouth to speak. Her lips quivered, not knowing what to say. The man grabbed his glass of whiskey and took a sip.

"Get out of my fucking house."

Those words stung worse the second time. Tears streamed down Marissa's face. This was her last chance to say she was sorry.

"Honey, I—"

"You heard what I said, didn't you?" Her husband stood up and walked forward. He stared down at his wife menacingly. "I said get out of my fucking house."

Marissa hugged him, hoping that that would change something. He pushed her away and splashed the rest of his whiskey in her face.

"Get out of my fucking house now, you miserable bitch!"

Marissa screamed as she turned around and ran to the front door. She jolted down the staircases, regretting once again that her husband's beliefs didn't align with her own.

She opened the door to the apartment building, rushed outside and walked down her crowded sidewalk. She reached the corner of the block, wiped her face and looked up.

Across the street, a replica of a familiar blonde smiled and waved.

At that moment, Marissa realized she was right where she belonged.

Chapter 10
Toilet

A slightly used condom reflected the waning summertime as Vera scuffled down a weedy sidewalk. The emasculated heat evaporated from the surface of its complex latex construction.

The ornately dressed brunette had her first bartender interview today smack dab in the middle of West Bubblefuck. The dried contraceptive fluttered in the mid-afternoon breeze.

As her expensive bow heels ambled toward their destination, thoughts of trepidation leaked into the girl's mind.

This was an opportunity she couldn't screw up.

Vera looked down at her sleek and modish smartphone. The place was just around the bend.

Nervousness pressed every inch of her body as she bumbled forward. Her heart started pounding, but she knew she could handle it. Behind her, the city's skyline reared its delusions of grandeur.

The candidate neared the hole of entry, the likes of which was surrounded by a thick, untrimmed bush. This bar looked like a rundown shack, but Vera tried not to judge too quickly. She chose to stay positive.

Vera inserted herself into the cabin and examined the interior. A flickering computer monitor sat in the right corner of the room. A door stood on the opposite wall. The rest of the space was empty.

She walked over to the screen and introduced herself, assuming the machine was some sort of virtual assistant.

"Good afternoon! My name is Vera. I believe I have an appointment with Christine?"

The computer happily responded. "Nice to meet you, Vera! I'll be there in a second."

The applicant rubbed her sweaty palms on her dress and folded them behind her waist. She smiled as her blonde interviewer swung open the door fast and extended a hand.

"I'm Christine, but everyone calls me Chrissy."

Vera shook her hand eagerly. "The pleasure is all mine, Chrissy." She looked her evaluator in the eyes and said, "I'm looking forward to getting to know more about you and your business."

Chrissy grinned back at the girl, clearly impressed by her confidence. "For sure! Let's go to the other room. I'll ask you a few questions there."

The jobseeker followed the Special through the doorway to a dilapidated dining room. She resisted covering her mouth when the stench of cheap beer and other liquids wafted into her nostrils. Chrissy sat down at a table with four chairs. Vera took a seat opposite her.

Fisticuffs held her head in her hand. "So, where should I begin?"

Vera folded her hands on the table and straightened her back. She was woefully underprepared for what came next.

✳✳✳

A bead of condensation eased down the side of a cool glass of whiskey. Vera stared at it with a squinting right eye.

The rest of her face was pressed down against the minibar in her garish apartment. Antidepressants filled the cap of a half-empty bottle of 94 proof alcohol.

The ghost of a man she loved pulled up a barstool and poured himself a drink. Vera turned her head slightly to acknowledge him. Nowadays, he was her most frequent visitor.

He noticed her newest white accessory on the counter. He swirled the ice cubes in his glass, took a sip and waited for his host to speak.

"I'm not engaged Dad, don't worry."

The man scoffed. "I sure as hell hope not. At the minimum, the guy has got to afford a half-decent ring."

Vera smiled and picked her head up off the counter. He always knew how to brighten the mood.

"So, are you actually seeing anyone at the moment? It's not that I want to know all about your business or anything. I just feel like I have to step in for your mother from time to time."

Vera looked down at her whiskey and shook her head. "No, not right now." She leaned in close enough to see her reflection in the glass. "I'm just looking for a job to pass the time."

Her father nodded. "I see."

The girl shrugged. "Maybe I should be looking for a husband instead. Someone with a well-paying career and lots of money." She sighed. "Being a housewife doesn't sound too bad."

"Stick with what you're doing." The man rotated his liquor slowly in a circle. "I think that fits you a lot better."

Vera looked to the ghost and sank her head back down on the minibar. "Yeah, you're right."

Her father chuckled. "Of course I'm right! Don't settle for what's comfortable." He placed his hand on his daughter's shoulder. "Aim as high as you can and you'll get far. I know it."

The prospect grabbed his hand and remembered every detail. "Thanks Dad."

Pops gulped down the rest of his alcohol and set his glass down on the counter. "Anytime, kiddo."

They rested there in silence for a while. Vera tried her best not to think of anything. She just wanted to enjoy the moment.

Her dad spoke first. "So what's with the ring? Are you part of a cult or something?"

Vera grinned and shook her head. "This company I'm applying for wants me to meet them at the bar down the road soon. They said I should put on the ring when I feel it's the right moment."

The man leaned back and raised an eyebrow. "What the hell is that all about?"

The candidate raised her hands and frowned. "I don't know, but I figured it's worth a shot. I have nothing else better to do tonight. Plus, drinks are on them."

Dad reached over to the whiskey and poured himself a second glass. He took a sip and smirked.

"How do you feel about the gig?"

Vera leaned back and chortled. "Honestly, I'm probably not going to take it if they offer it to me. Something about it doesn't seem right."

The man shook the ice rocks in his drink. "I don't blame you." He laughed. "That job sounds like it's for clowns."

***

Priscilla finished rubbing the lint off her glasses for the fifteenth time that early September morning. She needed to hurry. She didn't want to be late for her first day of high school.

The aspiring honors student stared at herself in her bathroom mirror, shaking with bits of fear and excitement. A new school meant new friends, new teachers and a new life. The best chapter of her childhood was about to begin.

She grabbed her schoolbag, walked out of her bathroom, bounced down the stairs and jumped out the door.

Priscilla nearly ran to the bus stop by her house. As her public transportation arrived, a whole new experience came with it. She sat on the seats closest to the door, looking outside at everything that rushed past her.

It wasn't long before the young girl found herself staring up at her new school. She skipped out the bus and strode up to the entrance, trying her best to keep composure.

She moseyed through a hallway and into a gymnasium where all the other freshmen sat anxiously on the bleachers. She took her place by a girl with big hair and waited for the assembly to begin.

"Hi!" Her neighbor extended a hand. "I'm Cassy. What's your name?"

Priscilla's eyes opened wide. She took the girl's hand in her own and responded softly. I'm P-P-Priscilla." Her face lit up like gunshots. "Nice to m-m-meet you."

The bashful student dug her head inside her uniform. She'd never had a friend before.

Little did she know, Cassy was going to make her next four years a living hell.

Sissy would remember them forever.

***

A young woman wearing a long tailcoat and pleated dress slouched asleep in a leather green accent chair. Her panoramic window greeted airships as they flew into and out of daybreak's view.

The sun contoured her innocence as she turned to the light. A grandfather clock ticked away in the otherwise dim living room. Mosaic lamps and vases glinted on fuzzy furniture. The thinly cut carpet laid undisturbed as the girl woke up to live the last moments of her life.

"Vera!" Her father's voice was the only thing she recognized beyond the shadow of a doubt. "Breakfast is ready!"

Vera's eyes opened to an unfamiliar world. The jobseeker stood up slowly and walked to her window. The cosmopolitan bustle on the other side of the glass looked wrong. Her mind told her not to trust her surroundings.

"Vera! Do I have to come and get you myself?"

Her heart told her she was right at home. Footsteps resounded behind a wooden door. Someone softly knocked.

"Princess, are you awake yet?"

Tears welled in Vera's eyes. Her entire body trembled. She didn't care if this was real or make-believe. She just wanted to see him alive again.

The girl wiped her face with her coat and cleared her throat. She tried to speak as best she could. "You may c-come in."

Dad swung the door open just as gracefully as she remembered. "Are you OK, honey?"

Vera ran and threw herself onto her father, smothering him with all the infinite love a daughter could muster.

The man returned the hug and smiled. "Who are you and what did you do with my child?"

The girl laughed as a tear streamed down her face. "Shut up."

It had been so long since she'd smelled his cologne. She barely spoke above a whisper.

"I'm not letting go ever again."

Dad patted her head. "Vera…"

She sank deeper into his off-white vest as several more tears ran down her cheeks. The man suddenly remembered why he was there.

"Our food is ready, sweetheart. Let's head downstairs before it gets cold, OK?"

Vera leaned away and cleaned her face with her sleeves again. She nodded and smiled. "OK, Dad." She looked into his eyes. "Thank you."

Dad chuckled. "Don't thank me yet! For all we know, it could taste horrible!"

The candidate folded her hands behind her back. "Yeah, you're probably right!" She needed this.

The pair walked down two flights of hardwood, their ancestors blessing them along portraits on the walls.

The kitchen smelled like smoked ham and biscuits. A cool breeze wafted in from a slit in a nearby window, turning pages in a freshly opened cookbook and mingling with the sunshine hanging over the matted island.

A sizzling heap of scrambled eggs sat inside a large dish on the counter. Breakfast had been served. Vera walked over and memorized every detail. She couldn't believe her father made this.

"Dad, this looks incredible."

The man walked to a cabinet and grabbed some forks and knives. "Thank you!" He offered the utensils to his daughter. "But how does it taste?"

Vera sat on a stool by the counter. She cut into the eggs, picked up a forkful and placed them in her mouth. "Holy crap." She covered her mouth to keep her breakfast from falling out. "Who are you and what have you done with my father?"

Dad laughed as he sat by his daughter. He winked and exclaimed, "You'll never find the body!"

✳✳✳

Mucus dripped onto yellow-brown toilet water as Priscilla fished for her spectacles in a bowl she knew too well. The left lens cracked during Cassy's latest onslaught.

She wiped her eyes with her sleeve before finally pulling her glasses out from underwater. She rested them on the tank.

Ten chipped fingernails trimmed the circumference of the commode as the redhead placed her soggy chin above a crusty outline of urine. She thought about having a new life. In this life, she'd be the bully.

She'd be the one having all the fun.

Priscilla lifted herself slowly. The cold water on her face leaked down her white blouse. She spun some toilet paper on her hand and dried what she could.

The redhead's smartphone vibrated in her pocket. She pulled it out and read a notification about another school shooting. The news reminded her of the semi-automatic sitting under her parents' bed. The one that she had thought of bringing to Cassy's house one night.

Later that week, Priscilla became the bully. From that point forward, she prided herself on having fun at other people's expense.

***

A pair of happy dress shoes descended a set of stairs as a doting father met his daughter by a sun-kissed foyer.

"How do I look?"

Vera's father twirled like a ballerina as the lint sprung from his plaid woolen vest and danced with the warm rays of light in the room. His daughter fell in love all over again.

She grinned and said, "Eh, I've seen better."

"Wow!" Dad bent over and tried to smooth out the wrinkles in his pants. "Way to hang your pops out to dry!"

Vera laughed and opened the front door. "You look perfect."

The man smiled, walked over and kissed the top of her head.

They stepped outside to a beautiful new reality in the sky. The townsfolk beamed from ear to ear as they walked down brick laid streets to friendly groceries, bakeries and newsstands. Gigantic clouds floated past them peacefully, obscuring the light blue sky behind them.

Vera looped her arm around her father's, savoring each whiff of his cologne as they ambled toward the nearest intersection. They stopped by a flower shop and admired the fresh lily bouquets on display.

"Your mother would've loved it up here." He paused as a florist arrived with a watering can. "You can smell adventure in the air."

Vera searched for the right words to say. She questioned why she'd woken up in this reality. Maybe it had something to do with the immoveable white ring on her finger.

For the most part, however, she wondered if there was any way she could stay. She wanted to enjoy as much time as she could with her father. If this was a dream, she wanted it to be reality.

Vera dug into her tailcoat pocket and found some silver coins there. She grabbed a few and offered them to the florist, then picked up a bouquet in her hand. The pair continued walking, flower petals softly floating behind them.

Dad looked over and smiled. "What's the occasion?"

His daughter smelled the flowers and exhaled loudly. "I just felt like it."

The man chuckled. "Living in the moment?"

Vera nodded. "Exactly."

Town hall's clock sat high above the center of the city. The prospect and her pops turned the corner and walked toward it. Minute and hour hands connected. A graceful chime reverberated throughout the drifting island's streets.

"Honey…" Vera could tell her father was choosing his words carefully. She saw him take a deep breath before continuing. "I wanted to talk to you about your medication."

The girl wondered if this conversation would transpire exactly the way she imagined on her minibar.

Vera turned her head and looked at her father. The sunlight sparkled in his light blue eyes. She realized instantly that nothing would have prepared her for this.

"I've been seeing a doctor since you've been gone." She turned her head down to the sidewalk, desperately hoping she could wrap her arms around him forever. "It's been helping me… a little."

Dad kept staring ahead as he spoke. "I know it's been hard." He nervously adjusted his vest. "I'm sorry… about everything."

Vera knew he was going to say that. She watched the ground in silence as her father cleared his throat.

"But I'm glad that you're trying your best to take care of yourself." The man turned to his daughter. "I'm happy you're trying to move on with your life, honey."

He paused, looked away and thought about his next words carefully. When he spoke again, Vera's fondest memories with him flashed in front of her eyes.

"The only thing I ask is that you please lay off the alcohol." The man audibly exhaled. "I only want the best for you." He smiled. "And alcohol tends to not bring out the best in us."

The jobseeker glanced at her father and turned away before tears welled in her eyes. She responded as best she could with a raspy voice.

"It's so hard, Dad. It's been so hard without you."

The man nodded. "I know, honey." He glimpsed down at his shoes as they shone in the afternoon light. "But you're moving forward, one step at a time."

The sound of the clock grew louder as they walked closer. Dad reached his arm over his daughter's shoulder and pulled her in close. Vera could smell his cologne wash over her.

"You've got a wonderful future ahead of you, kid." He kissed his child's head. "Everything will turn out just the way it should."

Vera nestled her head close to her father's chest. She spoke barely above a whisper.

"I love you so much, Dad."

The man leaned his head against his daughter's and whispered back, "I love you more, honey."

The pair walked by town hall's white alabaster steps and sat down by a metallic lion. The statue stared ahead as the waning sun cast orange hues along its frame.

The man and his daughter looked back at the long street they traveled on, each happy to have found one another. Dad leaned back and squinted as the sky splashed light on his face. He turned to Vera.

"A lot of good things are coming your way, honey." He grinned. "Just wait and see."

The clock above suddenly burst into pieces. Glass rained on the duo as a blonde, brunette and redhead dropped and landed in front of them, each wearing chiffon skirts and elegant kerchiefs.

"Miss, you slice 'em up on the left!" Blondie waved her arms forward. "Siss, you light 'em up on the right!"

"Yes ma'am!" The pixie-cut maiden grew a greatsword from the palm of her hand.

"Yee!" The pigtailed ginger swung two semi-automatic from her index fingers.

"On your marks." The leader pushed a leg back. "Get set." She leaned onto the ground.

The wide-eyed Vera struggled to understand what was going on. "What are you—?"

"Go!"

The black-haired vixen flew high into the air and landed by the florist. Upon her arrival, the shop owner's eyes grew red. She dropped the flowers in her hand and grew talons from her fingertips. Her mouth frothed with saliva as her teeth metamorphosed into fangs.

The creature swung its claws at the swordswoman, who promptly dodged and retaliated with her weapon. The florist was sliced into two immediately, just as business owners along the street transformed and ran toward their guests.

Opposite, the bouncy joker sprayed bullets into concrete and flesh as she laughed her way down the sidewalk. Blood from the stores seeped between bricks. Once she ran out of ammo, the comedian spawned a handful of grenades in her hands and chucked them at her enemies. The explosions launched bits of skin into the air.

Their leader punched holes through random citizens on town hall's front lawn, occasionally stopping to admire the work of her associates.

Vera gripped onto her father's arm on the steps, praying for a miracle. Her lilies rolled away with the wind, floating above gore and mangled corpses.

Tonight's shift had just begun. After the slaughter was over, the trio returned to town hall. Each had triumphant grins plastered on their faces.

The blonde raised a bloodied hand at the candidate and smiled. "Welcome to the next part of your interview, Vera!"

The dreamer squeezed her father's hand hard. "W-What is this, Chrissy?"

"It's kind of a long story." The interviewer shrugged. "But it's kind of what we do!"

Vera looked at Missy and Sissy and shook her head. "I d-don't understand."

Chrissy nodded. "You will after I explain it to you." She pointed at Vera's dad. "But before I get to that… who's that guy?"

Vera stood and jumped in front of her father. The man leaned back onto the steps, sweating from anxiety.

"He's my dad." The daughter spread her arms up in surrender. "I'm not s-sure what's going on, but please leave us out of it."

Chrissy looked back to Miss. The Conjurer frowned and shook her head. Fisticuffs breathed loudly and tried to negotiate.

"Vera, nothing here is real aside from me, you, Miss and Siss." She pointed up to the broken clock above them. "We wouldn't have been able to survive that fall if this was real, right?"

Vera followed the blonde's finger, her head and arms shaking with nervousness. "I don't care if this place is r-real or made-up." She tried to keep composure. "Just please leave us alone."

Chrissy tilted her eyes to the ground and placed a hand on her hip. "That's not how this works. We go into people's nightmares and help them wake up." She shrugged. "Right now, we're in your nightmare. Most of the time, we're in other people's nightmares."

Tears were welling in Vera's eyes again. Her knees were trembling from the stress. "I d-don't care." She sunk her head into her chest. "Just leave me here with my dad." She gasped for air. "It's all I ever wanted."

"Chris…" Missy pointed her sword at Vera's dad. "That guy… he's turning."

Vera swung her head back. Her father stared wide-eyed as the bones in his fingers sharpened and elongated dramatically. His skin grew with the bone, transforming his once human hands into strange claws.

The man looked up at his daughter as a red hue filled his eyes. Water leaked down his face as his mouth quivered. He never wanted to leave her side.

"Out of the way, Vera." Chrissy took a step forward. "We need to finish this."

The prospect yelled back. "Leave us alone!" She took another look at her dad. His body was convulsing in strange places. She continued standing in front of him, arms stretched wide. "I'm not letting you touch him!"

"I'll take care of it!" Sissy spun a shotgun out of nowhere. "Quick and easy!"

"Wait, Siss." Chrissy took another step forward. "Vera, this is your last chance. Step aside and let us end this. We'll explain everything afterward."

Vera shook her head. "No!" She took a third look at Dad. His transformation was nearly complete. "Just let me die here."

"It's now or never, Chris." The metamorphosed man lay motionless behind Vera. Missy pleaded. "We need to do this."

"Vera." Chrissy walked forward slowly. She climbed the first two steps and extended a hand. "Please listen to me. We're going to help you."

Daddy's girl looked down into the blonde's blue eyes and tried to discern if she was telling the truth. She turned around one last time and stared briefly at her dad's motionless body.

Vera closed her eyes, turned forward and began extending her hand toward Chrissy.

The monster spurred to life. He jumped and dug a claw into the girl's side. She yelped before a gunshot barked through the sky.

Dad slammed hard onto the alabaster. Vera fell on top of him, half her body embedded with metal.

Vera smelled her father's cologne as their blood intertwined and dripped down town hall's steps. She closed her eyes and drifted to sleep.

Her last wish became reality.

Chapter 11
Psycho

A ceiling fan spun viciously in a circle. Val's eyes grew numb from staring at the center of it.

Her simple white room contrasted sharply with the black, burning wound beneath her hospital gown. She turned her head and stared at the girl with the long, auburn ponytail sleeping in the bed next to her.

A part of her regretted every second that led her to that point. She blamed her lack of confidence, inexperience and cowardice. At the same time, she told herself she wasn't going to cry anymore.

Just as Val remembered her last conversation with Chrissy, Silvia opened her eyes for the first time in a while. She winced when she tried lifting her head from her pillow. Her body was numb from lying asleep for so long.

Val turned her head again and watched in silence as her new roommate came to terms with their situation. The redhead turned her head and noticed Val, then looked up at the ceiling with an emotionless expression.

Val spoke softly. "Welcome back from the dead."

The airbender thought about the conversation she'd have with Silvia when she woke up. She hoped it'd turn out similar to what she imagined.

A white ring and red ring sat on the drawer between them, faintly glinting in the fluorescent light. Silvia opened her mouth to speak, but couldn't find the right words to say.

Val didn't mind the silence. She closed her eyes and imagined her mother bringing her flowers and kissing her forehead.

After a few minutes, the pyromancer spoke with a croaky voice.

"Thank you for everything back there." She cleared her throat. "You saved my life. I owe you."

Val breathed in, breathed out and replied.

"I wish I could have done more." She shook her head, reminding herself not to shed a single tear anymore. "I'm sorry it ended this way."

Silvia coughed loudly. "Well, it could have been a lot worse." She turned to Val. "You know her right?"

Val sighed. "I thought I did, at least."

The former joshi kosei returned her gaze to the ceiling. "Why… why didn't she just kill us?"

That was the first question the windmaker had thought of when she awoke.

"She thinks this is all a game." Val clenched her fists underneath the sheets. "She wants us to play with her."

"So she's like Eliza then." Silvia closed her eyes. "A total fucking sociopath."

Val nodded. "Yeah, but at least she's obedient to Monica. Sissy… there's no rhyme or reason to her." She thought about the time she was nearly caught in the joker's shotgun blast, or when pigtail's grenades detonated a few feet away from her.

"She just does whatever she finds most fun."

Silvia scoffed. She turned her head in the opposite direction and tried to peek around the curtains hanging over a nearby window.

"I never should've agreed to any of this." It was raining out. "Monica took advantage of me when I was at my breaking point. She'll manipulate other girls until she gets what she wants." The redhead dug her fingernails into her mattress. "She needs to be stopped."

Val tried envisioning the world from Monica's point of view. She cared about gender inequality, too. Any woman can get behind that. She was tired of fearing the so-called man in the shadows, constantly looking over her shoulder late at night when her shift was over.

She thought about Chrissy and Missy. If they were alive, she would've loved to hear their opinions.

The new hire sat up and stood beside her bed. She lifted her mattress and pushed it off its frame. Bottles of amaretto, irish cream and rum were nestled in the center. She swooped all of the ingredients into her arms and dumped them onto the drawer.

She pulled out the first cabinet and dug her hand in the back. She pulled out two glasses with one hand and sat them nicely between herself and her roommate. Silvia looked at the display and raised an eyebrow.

"How the hell?"

"I snuck out the window a couple of times when you were asleep." Val moved the red ring over to the edge of the drawer. She shrugged.

Silvia picked up her ring and stared at it. She could feel hate boil in her digits. "So what's the plan?"

Val began pouring amaretto and rum into a glass. "We need to train every night until we're out of here." She reached for the irish cream next. "Then we go after Monica."

The redhead nodded. "And the crazy bitch?"

The airbender took a sip of her cocktail. "Leave her to me."

Chapter 12
Chicken Noodle Soup

Val penetrated through the wall of Class 1A fast, ricocheting off wooden desks before landing in the corner.

A trickle of blood stained her otherwise pure white private school uniform.

"You've got a lot more spunk now, don't you dear?"

The shadowy foreigner slowly rose from a pool of darkness by the chalkboard. She, too, wore a joshi kosei outfit, though her skirt was made up of black and white checkers.

Cross-armed, she looked Val's way with a smirk. "You don't suppose I've had anything to do with it?"

The breezy student kicked a current beneath her and pounced. Monica's right arm turned to black and elongated as she tried to spike the air wielder mid-flight. Val flipped onto her back and blew into the ceiling, landing on the tiled classroom floor before sweeping her leg to create a forward blast of wind.

Anticipating the mini-storm, her opponent attempted to fade into nothing. The gust, however, burrowed deep into her gut before she could escape, rocketing her back to the misery of Class 1B.

Val walked into the arena where their tussle began. She responded to Monica's query with clenched fists.

"I'm brave because I want to be."

Blood oozed from the cockney woman's lips as they lifted to form a smile. She hoisted herself up with a chair leg.

Her body turning to shadow again, she happily uttered, "You're welcome."

The new hire rushed forward. She reached the darkening girl in a little over a second, but the shadowmancer's form had entirely blackened by then. Val's fist had just missed Monica's vanished face.

Val closed her eyes and breathed in, breathed out. She couldn't afford to let her emotions take over.

She turned to the classroom door and turned its handle. A creepy, dim-lit hallway with no other doors greeted her outside. She took a step forward.

Horror smeared the floors of the seemingly abandoned high school. Val turned the corner to a hallway nearly identical to the first. With a gust of wind, she traveled forward to discover that all the passages ahead looked exactly alike.

As she scanned her surroundings to determine which direction she should head next, a flash of fire roared behind her.

"Fuck you!"

Silvia rushed into and out of view, screaming at an unknown enemy. Val did a one-eighty.

"Hey—!"

"I'll fucking kill you!"

The arsonist's hallway charred to black in the brief time it took the airbender to fly to her new partner. Drops of sweat ran down the firebender's white uniform blouse.

Val seized Silvia by the shoulder.

"Silvia! Enough! I think she's gone now."

The redhead wiped her brow with the back of her red-ringed hand. She spoke resentfully. "It was fucking Monica. She's playing with us." Embers ignited in her palm. "I'll burn that smile right off her fucking face!"

Val flicked the pyromancer's fire away with a snap of the wrist. "We'll get her. We just need to keep our cool."

Silvia looked Val in the eye begrudgingly before admitting, "You're right. I'll keep it under control."

The former trainee managed to muster a leader-like smile. "Good. Now which way did she go?"

"The party's right here, dear."

Monica levitated behind them with a grin, her likeness completely enveloped in nothingness.

Her mouth curled more as she stated, "You both have grown so much. I take great pride in that."

Silvia birthed a blazing spear in her normal hand and flung it at the shadow before Val had a chance to notice. It burned straight through Monica, darting down the shoddy hallway before crumbling into ashen pieces.

"You'd best mind your partner's advice more." A certain pixie-cut temperament came to mind. "Anger doesn't suit us girls well."

Tongues of fire singed off the ponytailed girl's hand instinctively. Val needed to maintain control for the both of them.

She stepped ahead of Silvia. "Are we finally going to settle this, Monica?"

The angel of death slowly lowered herself to the floor. She teased her bangs coquettishly and folded her arms behind her back. "I'd rather we stop fighting and talk, to be perfectly frank."

The ink on her body dissolved, as if conveying her innocent intentions. For a split second, the newbie bartender mistook this as genuine.

"What's there to talk about?" Val could sense the air around her stir as she recalled the memory of her friends. "I think you've given us enough monologues at this point."

"Oh, I'm sure you have everything sorted out by now." Monica lifted one finger and presented it before the pair. "If I may ask, however, what did become of that silly girl you were with?"

The hot hole in Val's chest burned as intensely as the flames sizzling from Silvia's appendages.

"My team will take care of her after we take care of you, of course." Monica smiled. "I hear she's quite vicious."

Val still couldn't make sense of Priscilla's motivations, but that didn't matter. "Once we're done with you, I'll take care of her myself."

"Will you now, dear?" Monica let out a brief chuckle. "And how exactly will you go about doing that on your own without a proper team?"

Val sneered.

"You don't have to worry about that."

Slightly disappointed, Monica looked down at her hand and saw the shadows creep into her fingers once more. "I'd have you know that both of you girls have impressed me, even if one of you has had a change of heart." She flashed a grin toward Silvia. "I may actually allow you both to live."

Wind and fire arched their backs, poised for whatever shitstorm lay ahead of them. The current picked up around Val's ankles and lifted her hair.

"This ends tonight, Monica."

"I'd like to think otherwise, dear." The black quickly flowed across Monica's body once more, transforming her likeness into a ghoul again.

Beyond her figure, pools of red liquid collected and swayed ominously down the hallway.

"The revolution has just begun, after all."

A rush of blood swallowed the foreigner's silhouette and crashed at the duo's feet. Val waved a hand to build an airstream.

"Move!"

She propelled Silvia backward, then blasted an incoming wave of blood before it consumed her. She launched herself toward her comrade and jutted around the next corner.

Another ocean of blood pounded the hallway before them. Silvia pointed to a double door entry behind them.

"There!"

Val spun a new gust of wind in her hands and flung the pyromancer and herself through the doorway into a large, empty cafeteria room. Silvia locked the doors before the mass of red caught up to them.

As the pair caught their breath, they took a moment to analyze the room they were in. Thin yellow stains oozed down the cafeteria's paneled off-white walls. Cobwebs connected each table to the seats adjacent to them, and a motor's humming could be heard coming from a room nearby. Most noticeable of all was a terrible odor emanating from the buffet.

Silvia pinched her nose and squinted. "What the hell is this fucking smell?"

Val headed over to the buffet. Buckets of brown, green and gray muck bubbled beneath a flickering heating lamp. For a moment, she had remembered the horrors she had witnessed in Missy's last nightmare. Now and then, she had to tell herself she was strong.

"It's this food. If you can call it that."

"Probably another one of Monica's tricks. Man, I can't wait to fucking disintegrate—"

"Silvia... remember what I said before about keeping our cool? We can't let her manipulate us."

Val spoke to Silvia's experience. "Right. You're right." Silvia clenched her fingers slowly. "No more emotion."

The humming motor outside grew slightly louder, as if it was given more to chew.

"Valorie..."

Silvia looked up at Val.

"Before shit hits the fan, I just wanted to say that I'm sorry for everything. You and me... we didn't deserve any of this."

Val looked down, desperately trying not to think of her mother. The discolored panels gluing the walls together started vibrating.

"No one deserves anything we've been through." She breathed in, breathed out. "But we're stronger than anything life throws at us."

One by one, the panels sprang off. The roof above transformed into a thin layer of dirt, then blew away as a cacophony of metallic noises and an unbearable heat invaded the cafeteria.

When each wall had broken down, Val and Silvia finally understood the kind of nightmare they were in.

In every direction, pitch dark girls and boys were fed into monstrous, reddish-brown machines via conveyor belts. These automatons produced heaps of chunky soup with the bodies, then spluttered the liquid into gigantic canisters on the wretched factory floor.

Each dish at the buffet bubbled out of its tray, as if it had wanted to return to the depths from which it came. Monica squatted over the edge of a rumbling machine high above Val and Silvia. She laughed heartily.

"Quite lovely, isn't it?"

Before she had a chance to reply, Val was knocked forward with a shockwave. Tiny bolts illuminated the chrome floor she fell onto.

Two bright yellow ponytails bounced on the opposite end of the cafeteria.

"It's electrifying!"

A tall flame combusted in Silvia's human hand as Val pushed herself off the floor. Val placed her hand on the redhead's shoulder.

"I've got the short one. Go take care of Monica."

The fire in Silvia's palm danced higher than ever. "With pleasure."

Silvia launched a sharp blast of flame through the machine that Monica stood on, causing it to explode immediately. In the same moment, Val jumped into the air and dropped a mini maelstrom on Eliza.

The loli somersaulted off the ledge and landed on a conveyor belt. The shadowmancer permeated through the blast and floated to a motor nearby. Val and Silvia made haste.

Silvia's soles illuminated bright red as she blasted flames off her feet and soared up to Monica's machine. When she flew over the edge, she rocked another fireball toward the cross-armed Monica and decimated another one of those terrible engines.

Monica dissolved through the explosion again and extended a shadowy arm to a conveyor belt above. As she sprang upward, her hand blackened into oversized spikes and threw themselves toward Silvia, who was still suspended in midair.

The scarlet jerked herself away with a blast, ricocheting herself to the top of a bumbling engine. The spikes crashed into several machines at once, each of them exploding upon impact.

Monica smirked from the high ground. Both her hands transformed into spikes and dived to where Silvia stood below.

Frantically, the redhead directed all the heat in her body to her right arm and raised her hand toward the onslaught. A sloppy beam erupted from her palm, destroying most of the spikes before they hit her. A few, however, managed to slip past the counterattack and sliced open Silvia's shoulder, stomach and ankle.

The beam carried on and melted the platform where Monica stood, but failed to do any damage. Silvia yelled in pain after the fire left her palm, gripping the spot on her stomach where her enemy's attack had hit.

She knew that she couldn't stop for long. As her hand recovered, she sipped some alcohol from a flask she kept in her skirt's waistband. Then, in a swift motion across her chest, she produced a blazing crimson sword dripping molten lava. She was ready again.

Using her feet, Silvia propelled herself up to the moving walkway where Monica stood. She caught a glimpse of the rocker grinning before bringing her blade down onto her head. Monica dodged effortlessly, then turned to shadow before Silvia could follow up with more swings. She floated backward, then shaped her arms into two gigantic scythes.

Monica launched her right arm quickly, but Silvia deflected the move with her sword. The other scythe followed close behind.

Silvia swung up and blocked the weapon's blade before it could hit, but destroyed her sword in the process.

Undeterred, Silvia launched herself high again, directing the heat into her right arm a second time. She blasted several streams of fire toward the shadow girl, demolishing the conveyor belt instantaneously. She was sure her last-minute maneuver paid off.

A sliver of black shot out of the explosion. Monica appeared right in front of Silvia before the latter could notice. Her right hand mutated into an absurdly-sized hammer and knocked Silvia straight in the face while in midair, catapulting her through a motor below and onto another conveyor belt filled with blank-faced children.

As the assembly line creaked onward, the tired Silvia began to lose hope.

Beneath her, Val chased Eliza from one machine to the next. The loli sprinkled a few shocks behind her to keep her pursuer busy, but Val knew she was up to no good.

Eliza landed on a conveyor belt, then sprinted straight into the mouth of one of those murderous machines. Val stared intently while clinging onto the edge of an oversized engine above.

The churning contraption lit up in a flash of electricity. Its usual rumbling grew louder as its metal parts rearranged themselves. The opening where it had formerly swallowed children grew steel teeth, and the top portion of the machine spawned a set of luminescent eyes. Rusted miniature arms and legs spread from its sides and bottom. The newly sentient being seized and chomped down on the platform it once fed on, then sprang upward to crunch Val.

Val pushed herself back in time. She had suspected Eliza had something up her sleeve, but was quite surprised to discover the little girl's abilities had grown so drastically. The airbender reassured herself that she had improved significantly, too.

With a clap of her hands, a tornado unleashed itself upon the monster and disassembled its metallic body.

Two more of these beasts popped up behind Val, mouths agape. She jumped high and punched a current straight into one of the robot's throats, then kicked an airstream into the right side of the other assailant.

Before both could batter into the bubbling canisters below, a trio threw itself toward Val in midair while her back was turned. As the closest chomped down, Val blew some wind to launch herself slightly above it, then commanded the air to squeeze the other two assailants together. She lifted off the first machine and watched as its two comrades collided into it.

Val threw a gust in front of her and maneuvered to another conveyor belt. She scanned the area for Eliza.

"Hewwo!"

Liza rode atop a machine larger than all the others combined. As its mouth grew wider, Val could see pools of billowing broth boil beneath its tonsils.

Val aimed an airstream straight for the left corner of the beast's mouth and unhinged it from the rest of its body. She kicked into the sky before the automaton bulldozed her, then pummeled it with a squall before it could lift its head. Eliza bolted away before Val's counterattack landed.

Seemingly out of nowhere, five more regular-sized machines descended onto the corpse where Val floated down to, undeterred by their brethren's failure. Liza giggled as they passed her in midair.

The loli couldn't keep this up forever. There's a strict limit to how much alcohol a girl her size could consume.

Like all the rest, the airbender made quick work of the machines. Val punched a hole straight through the first, then walloped the second into the third. She rocketed over the last pair and gusted them powerfully into the heap of broken parts below. Her training with Silvia had paid off.

Val threw a current in front of her and blasted herself to the next machine Eliza landed on. Just before the munchkin had a chance to transform another automaton, Val knocked her back with a sharp gust of wind. Instead of retaliating, Liza bounded away to an engine in the distance, sparks flying behind her.

Val noticed Liza's electricity was growing fainter. She paused to take a sip from her liquor tin. Eliza patiently waited for her next move, grin beaming and eyes twitching.

"You're wearing yourself out," Val slipped her flask back into her skirt pocket. "You need to stop before the alcohol takes over."

"Shut up!" Liza's hands curled like claws high over her head. A web of lightning spawned above her. She spread out her legs and lifted one slightly off the ground. "You're not going to stop us from having our fun! I'm gonna toast you, and then I'll get that murdering jokester too!"

Val closed her eyes. Thoughts of her former teammates swirled inside her head. Chrissy, Missy… Sissy. She wished she could go back in time to prevent this series of events from happening.

She breathed in, breathed out. She barely spoke above a whisper. "Whatever."

"Ragh!"

A bolt ignited Val's engine immediately, but she anticipated the attack and dodged milliseconds before it connected. Eliza's arms filled with flashing light and a barrage of electric bullets discharged from her palms.

Val jetted forward, her feet barely avoiding the onslaught behind her. She curved in the air, narrowly avoiding the stream of static, then shot herself straight up to Liza's machine. She cloaked herself in a bubble of wind before rushed headfirst into the automaton. It exploded before the little one could jump.

As she hurled below, Eliza screamed, "Get her!"

A half-dozen machines nearby quickly transformed and tossed themselves into the fray. They chomped into the smoke just as Val cast herself away with another current. After landing on a platform nearby, she noticed that one of them had managed to devour her shoe.

The six beasts stared as a seventh automaton caught up to them. An aggravated Eliza rode atop its head.

Before issuing her next command, she dipped into her shirt and drank the last drops of her Sex on the Beach. She threw the canister into the soupy depths below.

"Fucking crybaby! You're gonna… you're gonna die!"

Slouched over, breathing heavy, the loli drew a pointed finger up to Val one last time. She directed all of her energy to the tiniest point on her index.

Her drooling machines clenched their gears, waiting to pounce on Val's body once it had roasted. Val squinted her eyes and tried to focus. Something in the air was wrong.

She noticed Silvia had stopped fighting.

Eliza's cannon blasted, its booming noise reverberating through the factory. Wires and engines exploded. Steel twisted and light bulbs shattered.

Val dropped onto the conveyor belt. Smoke billowed from the left side of her body.

Her left arm was charred black.

Eliza's machines jauntily leaped to feed on their dinner. The brat sank into the last automaton as it moved toward Val slowly. She was exhausted, but proud of what she had managed to accomplish.

Eyes wide, Val desperately tried to clench her left hand. The feeling was worse than pain. It was devoid of anything.

The first machine pounced, mouth agape.

In a last-ditch move, Val kicked an airstream straight into its face.

With her right hand, she blew a small current behind her and lifted into a standing position. As the other machines closed in, she swirled a vortex that caused them to collide into one another. Then she threw her right leg and right hand back, blasted herself off the belt and rushed straight ahead to the half-conscious Eliza.

A tempestuous fist sank deep into the loli's mouth before she had time to realize Val had survived. Liza's body flung like a ragdoll until it broke through an assembly line and crashed into a lonely machine below.

The electrocutioner's body gradually slipped off the surface as the automaton's vibration purred on. With one eye open, she stared at the soupy canisters and wondered what she wanted to do with her life.

Eliza's body fell straight toward the broth, but Val caught it midair. She kicked back up to the machine.

Val lay Liza down as carefully as she could with one arm, glancing at her yellow ring as it flickered. She was alive, but needed help badly.

"You… can take it."

The hollow-eyed loli could barely speak above a whisper. "I'm… not having fun anymore." Her gaze drifted off. "I don't want… to be a part… of this."

For the first time, Val and Eliza agreed on something.

"I… don't want to be a part of this either." The windmaker grasped Eliza's cold hands. "But I'm going to do what's right."

The girl with hair drills managed to muster a smile. For a moment, it wasn't hard to imagine the two girls as friends.

"You're not… a big crybaby… after all."

Val removed Eliza's ring, and the loli was never seen again.

***

Silvia pushed herself off the conveyor belt's cheap rubber, her head spinning from her last pummeling. Monica oozed onto the platform from above, her shadow twisting into odd shapes before it stood upright. The black dissolved, revealing her true mischievous self.

"I've got to be honest here." One-by-one, Monica's fingers blackened and elongated. "When I first discovered you on that street, I saw a lot of myself in you."

Silvia couldn't let Monica get inside her head. She took out her liquor tin and downed the rest of her Fiery Apple. She was going to end this madness before it got any worse.

"Damaged. Abused. Mistreated, as if you were some kind of animal." Monica shook her head. "We hurt that man not for you, but for every woman out there."

The redhead looked down into her hands. "It's senseless, Monica. Violence is an endless cycle." She clenched her fists as best she could. "I know you have good intentions, but this isn't the right way to spread a message."

Her opponent giggled. "My plan will end when every man burns in the misery he sowed himself."

She extended a hand to Silvia.

"Come back to me, dear. Let's let the patriarchy wallow in the grief it rightly deserves."

Hateful memories spiraled in Silvia's mind. Her stalker's disgusting aftershave suffocated her.

"*Silvy…*"

The redhead ignited a high flame in her hand.

"That's right, sweetheart. Let's burn it down, toge—"

A fireball cooked past Monica's head, singeing her bangs clean off. She gasped, wiping a shadowy claw over her face to prevent herself from becoming bald.

Silvia tossed around another orb of flame in her hand.

"We all let hate consume us sometimes." She remembered her boring life. Taking the train, going to school, working late. "It's easy to give in to your negativity."

Val soared up from below and landed beside Silvia. She pointed her right fist back and aimed it at the shadowmancer. "Sometimes people need to be saved from themselves."

Monica looked at the pair incredulously, her grin now a grimace. "These drunkards don't deserve salvation."

"That may be the case." Val breathed in, breathed out. "But we'll be there for them anyway."

Monica's back arched. Her hands turned pitch black. Frustration painted her face a grayish color.

"You'll end up like every other foolish girl out there. Used up and tossed aside like trash!"

"Whatever the case may be," Val and Silvia pushed aside the pain.

"At least us girls have each other."

Monica clasped her hands over her head and formed a giant mallet. It grew into the air and threw itself toward Val and Silvia.

The former flew back, the latter sprinted forward. Silvia spawned a fiery spear in her hand and pierced Monica's darkened arms in midair, disconnecting the mallet from the rest of the shadow's body. It dissolved before it could hit the conveyor belt.

Before Monica could react, Silvia scalded her human hand and blasted a beam of fire. The blaze passed through the enemy's torso without a scratch, but Val had anticipated this. She leaped high in the air and threw a fist of wind toward Monica's skull, knocking her through the platform and into an engine below.

Val and Silvia pursued the warmonger without a word, eager to end her ambitions. Monica stood up from the fall and extended her colossus hands to two machines nearby. She tore them from their wiring and launched them toward her descending opponents. "Ragh!"

Val blew a current with her right hand and narrowly avoided the heap of metal as it skid across her charred left arm. Right behind her, Silvia summoned her molten red chains and cast a lasso around the second pile. She pulled it once it flew behind her, rocketed it over her head and crashed it straight into the exasperated Monica.

The engine exploded alongside several other automatons nearby. Val hurled a whirlwind into the carnage for good measure. Monica's sooty body twisted through the smoke and struck the cafeteria floor hard.

Val formed another bubble to protect herself and Silvia as they floated through the blast and landed on the surface where their fight began.

Monica struggled to stand up straight. Black spots covered her body and ink dripped off her fingers. Blood soaked her uniform.

"Women… deserve to be free."

She pulled out a tin from her bosom and furiously consumed all its contents. She threw it on the ground once empty, then produced another and downed some more.

"All men… are pigs."

Val and Silvia watched in disbelief as Monica tossed this can and began drinking a third, her body growing more black and changing shape with every gulp.

"They'll die… you'll die!"

The last tin's liquor spilled onto Monica's shirt as she dug two razor-sharp claws through the cafeteria's steel flooring.

"It'll all… die!"

The rest of her form contorted in every direction, expanding rapidly and crushing the soupy buffet.

Val and Silvia stepped back to the edge of the platform, gazing wide-eyed at the metastasizing spectacle in front of them.

The mass detonated. Val gripped Silvia's shoulder and kicked off into the air. A zigzag of spikes furiously cut their way to them.

One sliced Val's leg before she landed on another platform nearby. She winced as they landed on a motor.

Val turned to Silvia and screamed. "Go!"

The scarlet shot into the air before two spikes dug into her. She skidded on a generator nearby, then used her hand to soar straight ahead. The spikes followed her closely, exploding every mechanism in their wake.

Val hopped fast in the opposite direction as another collection of spikes gave chase. She peered down to Monica's grotesque shape below. It kept expanding.

She tossed a blow to the fiend while trying her best to keep her pace. Her current chopped a bubble off its head, but it grew back quickly.

Silvia noticed Val's efforts and sank a few flames into the beast's body. Each hole was swiftly filled with ink.

Undeterred, the pair aimed more wind and fire at the disfigured blob, carefully making sure to avoid the barbs that followed inches away.

The battlefield began collapsing onto itself as the crazed spikes shattered every machine in their path. Val threw another punch at the menace's head.

The shadow rolled back to reveal Monica's unconscious human form.

"Silvia!"

Val yelled to her partner across the fray, but the redhead had already noticed. She poured her energy into a ball of fire and propelled herself down to the beast.

Two spikes shot out of the demon's cranium and sunk themselves deep into Silvia's stomach. Suspended in the air, she aimed her fireball at Monica's human face and emitted the strongest beam of fire she had left in her.

The huge blast raged into the monster, boiling its head in an incalculable heat. Silvia directed more energy into the discharge even as five spikes buried themselves in her back and passed through to her front.

"Fuck… you!"

Blood oozed out Silvia's mouth as her flame grew more intense. She smiled realizing that she had broken the mold in spades.

Val stared as she continued hopping forward. The spikes behind were failing to keep up. She jabbed an airstream at the prongs while at a safe distance and they twisted and cracked before coming to a complete halt.

The shadow protecting Monica gradually spilled into a liquid on the cafeteria's surface. The rest of the blob's body grew clear blisters and popped, sloshing onto the remains of the billowing machines around it.

Silvia's fingers charred and cracked. Her pinky and thumb dissolved into the inferno, but the heat continued to climb.

Monica's body finally flung out of the mass, completely blackened by the fire Silvia had ignited on it.

When the flame from Silvia's palm extinguished completely, her dead eyes looked down upon her greatest accomplishment.

Chapter 13
Mom's Spaghetti

A tempest roared through the skies of the cruel, misshapen city. Raindrops pounded Val's yellow raincoat as she lurched across an empty cobblestone intersection downtown. She stopped in front of a window with a bright neon sign that spelled 'Barcade.' The hole in her chest burned. She breathed in, breathed out and stepped inside.

Val noticed the joker's insatiable smile and bright red pigtails when she dragged an unconscious, severely charred Monica through the streets one night prior. The rocker lay in Val's bed now, her breath barely above a murmur. Val spent hours searching alleyways to find her.

All that remained of Silvia was a red ring. Val knew from experience that her body wouldn't return to the real world. The ponytailed girl's final resting place now lay in the mind of a drunkard no one knew.

Val tried hard not to think about it. Her eyes still hurt from last night. She entered the bar briskly.

The airbender stood by the doorway and analyzed every corner of the room. She could barely hear the bouncer as pinball machines and rhythm games exploded with lights and high-pitched sounds.

"ID please."

Val passed him the card, her pupils still scanning every inch she could see. For a moment, she envied the drunk dreamers that tiptoed merrily across the arcade's creaky wooden floor. A part of her wished that she could have that life one day.

"Thank you."

He waved a hand to indicate she could enter. She did so cautiously.

Val winced each time she stepped forward. Her body was still exhausted. She stuffed her left hand in her pocket so Sissy wouldn't poke fun at her.

The interviewee swayed to the bar and pulled out a stool. She looked across the counter to see if her target had already started drinking. She spotted a few empty glasses on the opposite end, but no sign of the redhead anywhere.

An eyepatched bartender strolled in from the swinging door behind the bar. Her face lit up as soon as she saw Val in front of her.

"Hey buddy!"

Sissy bounced over to Val with a grin plastered on her face. Val couldn't shake the feeling that this chick had somehow grown even more deranged.

The gun-toting vixen sensed her former colleague's unease, but continued speaking anyway. She placed her hands firmly on the counter in front of Val, looked the windmaker in the eye and said, "So how are you?"

Val tried hard to stare back at her next opponent. She looked down and barely spoke above a whisper.

"Why did you…?"

Tears swelled in her eyes. She had once considered this person a partner. Now she was just another obstacle.

"Why did I… what?"

Val's mind was racing. She didn't want to think anymore. She just wanted to make her mother proud.

She placed her right hand over Sissy's left. It was all going to end tonight, one way or another.

Val cleared her throat, breathed in and out slowly, and tilted her head up. She returned Sissy's glare.

"I thought you were on our side."

The scarlet continued beaming her ridiculous smile. She chuckled a little before she spoke.

"Silly! I'm not on anyone's side!"

Sissy moved her hand out from underneath Val's and grabbed four shot glasses from the counter. She reached down and picked up three more with her right hand. She placed all seven in the small space between herself and Val, then turned around to get the alcohol.

A single tear streamed down Val's face as, one by one, Sissy filled each shot glass with yellow tequila. In her head, she told herself that she was about to do the right thing.

Sissy seized her first glass and stared at Val again. "Everything I do is for fun!"

As she downed the first shot, Val picked one up with a frown. She never found much sense in Sissy, but maybe that was the point.

Val drank her tequila in one gulp as her enemy moved on to her second.

"Is that why you shot me? Because you thought it'd be funny?"

Sissy's lips curled up as she swallowed her drink. She wiped her mouth with the back of her hand and said, "Exactamundo! Wasn't it exciting?"

The heat around Val's wound started to boil. The airbender was starting to lose her patience.

She scarfed down her second shot and picked up her third. Sissy grabbed her third, too.

"Something like that." Val looked at her reflection in the pool of yellow. "I'm planning on doing something exciting myself."

She filled her throat with that warm liquor and, without hesitation, snatched the seventh and last glass and swallowed that, too.

"Do you want to know what that is?"

Sissy tilted her head, a shot glass full of liquor still swirling in her hand.

Val forced a smile at Sissy.

"I'm going to kick your ass."

She pulled out a white ring from her pocket, slipped it onto her ring finger and vanished.

Sissy giggled. "That's what I like to hear!"

She guzzled her last bit of tequila, slipped on her red ring and disappeared in pursuit.

***

At first, Val couldn't tell if her eyes were open. She stood up carefully and looked all around her. Darkness engulfed every inch of this nightmare.

She placed one foot in front of her. The ground was hard and smooth. She walked forward slowly, listening for anything that may help her find a way out.

After traveling for a few minutes, Val bumped her nose against a dead end. She placed her hand against the wall. It felt lifeless, cold.

She stepped back and blasted a surge of wind in front of her. It broke the glass barrier instantly. Val couldn't help but think of her own nightmare when she saw those shards scatter.

She squinted her eyes as she walked through to the other side. The cobblestone alleyway in front of her was painted almost entirely white. Faint black lines were drawn around windows, gutters and bricks on the ground, but the scene was otherwise devoid of any color.

Val looked down at her outfit. No surprises this time. Although that, inofitself, was a surprise. She wore the same yellow raincoat from before.

She continued moving forward, placing her feet down softly. She studied her environment more once she made it to the end of the path. The road it connected looked the same, with windows, doors, streetlights and traffic lights appearing as if they had been drawn with a thin marker. Everything seemed so empty.

Tiny footsteps echoed from around the corner. Val placed her head against the wall, listening to the steps as they grew louder.

She crouched and took a peek at whomever was approaching. Down the sidewalk, a little girl in a fitted school dress clung onto her backpack straps tightly as she sauntered her way home.

As the girl moved closer, the windjammer could make out a metal band logo on the student's strap. Val immediately lost focus.

A pair of heels slammed loudly onto the stone. Sissy stood proudly in her bartender uniform, shooting a smile at the horrified

Val. She conjured a handgun in her right hand and pointed it at the little girl on the sidewalk. She chuckled before claiming:

"This is gonna be easy!"

Val shook her head back into place and waved a cyclone toward the middle of the street. The trajectory of Sissy's bullet was thrown off slightly, hitting the storefront just behind the student. Val jumped into the sidewalk and sprang ahead fast.

She threw herself over the young Monica. A second bullet grazed her right shoulder.

Val's eyes watered from the pain, but she wiped away her tears immediately. She tilted her head and looked at the little girl in her grasp. Monica's mouth was wide open, her mind still trying to make sense of what had just happened.

Val turned her back and yelled at the kid. "Climb on!"

The foreigner closed her mouth and stared.

"Now!"

Monica placed her arms around Val's neck without a word. The airbender kicked off high into the air just as shotgun fire ricocheted beneath them. Before she lost speed, she shot a rush of wind in front of her and launched Monica and herself across the bleak city.

Sissy's mouth curled up in a huge grin as she watched Val escape with the little girl in midair.

Val skidded on a four-story rooftop, holding onto the kid's arms so she wouldn't fly off. Once they came to a full stop, Monica let go and backed away to the edge.

As our main gazed at the petrified child, her horror quickly morphed into pity. At that moment, she swore to herself she would help the unconscious shadowmancer find a way out of her blackout, despite everything she took from her.

Val kneeled in front of little Monica. "Hi! My name's Valorie. What's your name?"

The third-grader looked behind her. For a person her size, it was a long way down. She addressed the woman in a low voice.

"I'm M-M-Monica."

Val smiled warmly. "It's very nice to meet you, Monica." She placed her uncharred hand on the girl's shoulder. "I hope we get to be good friends one day."

Val moved her palm down Monica's arm and grasped her small hand. "I'm going to get you out of here, OK?"

The student frowned, tears welling in her eyelids. Her mouth quivered. She couldn't find the courage to speak.

"You have to trust me." The air around the pair started to feel a little lighter. "We'll end this nightmare together."

Monica cleaned her face with her sleeve and looked into Val's eyes. Very quietly, she replied.

"O-O-OK."

Three hand grenades popped into the air behind the girl. Without hesitation, Val pulled Monica close to her chest and pushed away with a current. They flew back just in time.

The explosives detonated, engulfing the rooftop with a dark cloud. Val whipped up some more wind in her right hand and tossed it forward. The smoke parted, and Sissy stood in the middle.

Patchy flung a semiautomatic rifle over her right shoulder and snapped a submachine gun into her left hand. She smirked at the pair in front of her.

"Looks like somebody had a *little* too much to drink!"

"Sissy!"

Val stepped in front of the foreigner and tried to plead with the madwoman. "This is Monica's nightmare. Yesterday she tried to—"

She suddenly remembered Silvia's hanging corpse.

"Nani? What she do?"

Val looked back at little Monica behind her. For a second, she questioned whether she was making the right choice.

"Monica tried to kill me yesterday in another nightmare, but she wound up drinking too much and went unconscious." Val looked down at the blank surface beneath her feet. She breathed in, breathed out. "She's not a threat anymore. She doesn't need to be involved in this."

Despite her looks, Sissy wasn't the type to let grudges disappear so quickly. She chuckled.

"Murdering her is going to be so much fun! Yay!"

A breeze picked up around Val's ankles. Our heroine prepared for the worst.

"No one's going to kill anyone anymore, Sissy. No more vio—"

Sissy lifted the submachine gun and pressed down hard on the trigger. Val pivoted around and shielded Monica with her body, grasped the girl's hand and rushed up into the air with her right foot.

The pigtailed firearm aficionado shouted from below. "No way, José!"

She pointed the rifle with her other hand and sprayed more bullets at the duo. Val kicked into the sky and rushed into the alley below. The breezy hero breathed a cloud before she crashed into the pavement. She landed softly on her feet with Monica in her grasp.

As her cloud dissipated, Val noticed that the black lines in the alleyway were inching toward the walls on either side. They coagulated where each wall met the ground, bubbling like a grotesque wound.

Val didn't give it much thought. She and Monica sped ahead into the street with a sharp gust of wind.

Sissy skipped to the corner edge of the building above, humming merrily while waving her two guns. She aimed both at the pair below.

Bullets danced behind Val as she hurdled forward. She witnessed the neighborhood lose its outline as more black lines collected in pools on the street.

The joker tossed away her weapons and jumped to the ground below. She dug out a rocket launcher from her back pocket and promptly shot a missile toward her prey.

Val turned around with Monica once they arrived at the end of the street. She noticed the projectile and waved a draft. The wind exhausted the fire behind the rocket's tail, causing it to decelerate and roll. It stopped over a pool of black and sank inside slowly.

The air-wielder tried to appeal to the clown once more. She could make out Sissy's crazed smile even at a distance.

"Stop it, Siss! This doesn't make any sense." Val took a pause, then shouted, "This isn't what Chrissy would have wanted!"

Pricilla's grin grew wider. She joyfully proclaimed, "It's a good thing she's dead, then, isn't it?"

Val decided she had enough.

She let go of Monica's hand and spun a mini-twister in her right palm. "I don't know why you're doing this." The tornado grew higher and higher. It began to turn violently. Val's hair lifted in the air. "I just hope you're satisfied."

The avatar launched her tempest down the street. At that moment, Sissy thought about the girl who humiliated her. She cried in that bathroom almost every day.

Getting to witness Cassy go insane was more than worth the price of becoming a magical alcohol girl.

Sissy popped a laser sword over her head and cut through the vortex in one swipe.

The pools of black began traveling toward one another slowly and combined into larger masses on the cobblestone. Val and Sissy both noticed, but neither cared.

"You don't know me."

The hum of Sissy's new toy was the only thing that could be heard in that white void. The comedian's trademark smile had disappeared.

"I don't care about salvation or morals or being a good person." She dropped her sword. "That stuff is boring."

Patchy reached into her back pocket and pulled out a tin of booze. She took a sip, put away her liquor and summoned a ray gun into her hand.

"You can keep pretending you're a hero, but no one really cares." She walked forward. "I gave up on that a long time ago."

A bead of sweat rolled down Val's forehead. Monica took a few steps back.

"You're still kinda new, so you probably haven't realized," Sissy stepped on a large black pool of goo in the street. "Nothing ever really changes."

All of the lines that gave the world definition gathered here. A smile softly grew on Sissy's face.

"It's the same thing, over and over and over and over again."

Val crouched. Monica placed her arms around her neck without a word.

"We might as well have fun with it, right Val? We might as well lose our fucking minds!"

Sissy's heels sloshed through the black ink. By the time she walked through the pool, her massive grin had returned.

"So how about we have some fun, huh? Forget about the lying and the dying and the friendship and the virtues and let's just have some good old-fashioned fun!"

The redhead stood a dozen feet away from the pair now. She steadily lifted her ray gun.

"Not every story needs a goddamn hero anyway."

The pool began bubbling fast, as if it was boiling. Sissy looked behind her before pressing the trigger. "What the hell is that all about?"

Val used the distraction as an opportunity to fly high onto the building above. Priscilla looked back with a disappointed expression.

"Running away again? You can be such a drag sometimes!"

She shot a bright beam of energy at the duo. Val pushed away just before she and Monica were vaporized.

"Don't worry, Sissy. We'll definitely have fun tonight."

Val grabbed Monica's arms and set her down on the roof. She turned around to address the pigtailed menace again.

"But I'll be the only one laughing."

Sissy's face lit up. "That's what I like to hear!" She raised her ray gun once more.

Before she could fire, something grabbed her ankle. She looked down to discover a black, humanoid creature smiling up at her. Its empty white eyes and ridiculously large grin were filled with ill intent.

"Yuck!"

The scarlet stomped on the being's head and it exploded. Its body melted into goo and seeped back to the giant pool of boiling nothingness.

Once the being's mass was absorbed, the puddle grumbled. Sissy smirked.

"Looks like we're going to have a party!"

A massive two-dimensional circle rose from the pool. A long, slender body followed. The tower grew taller than any other lamppost, building, alleyway or street in this world of oblivion. Once it had finished growing, two white circles rotated into existence on its face. An absurd, cartoonish grin brightened across its image.

The monster's eyes and mouth illuminated the trio below. It bent lower and lower, opening its smile wider and wider as it approached the duo on the rooftop first.

Monica stared at the being in horror, tears streaming down her tiny face. The man in the shadows had manifested. It was her ultimate nightmare.

The future Conjurer ran. Val jumped in front of the creature's creeping face and punched an airstream toward it. The wind bounced off the demon's body. It continued its descent unscathed.

Monica stopped at the opposite edge, waiting for Val to help her escape. The windmaker kicked off to catch up to the girl.

Sissy beat her to the punch.

The jester shot a beam of light from above the beast's head. It dug through Val's burnt shoulder, causing her to skid along the rooftop. She screamed in agony.

Priscilla landed right in front of Monica and pointed her ray gun directly at the girl's face. The shadowy devil inched closer, its grotesque smile unflinching.

"Let's see…"

The firearm aficionado bounced her weapon playfully against her noggin. "Do I feed you to that thing, or do I shoot you myself?"

"Please…"

Still writhing in pain, Val crawled her way to Sissy and Monica. She pleaded one last time.

"Sissy… you don't have to do this."

"Really?" The redhead pointed to the fiend merrily levitating toward them. "Because if I don't shoot mini-Monica now, you're gonna die!"

Val stopped to catch her breath. She breathed in, breathed out. "That's fine." Chrissy taught her to prepare for the worst. "She deserves to live."

She weaved a current beneath her right hand and pushed herself to a standing position. Blood soaked the entire left side of her raincoat.

"We all fear something, Monica. But fear… doesn't define us."

Monica dried her tears and listened.

"It's what we do with that fear… that matters."

Sissy pressed her smoking gun directly on the girl's forehead.

"When I'm afraid… I tell myself something very important."

The gun's ray sensor burned.

"Fear is only as deep…"

But Monica could hear Val's words now more than ever.

"…as your mind allows."

Ink seeped into the little girl's right hand.

"You're stronger than you think, Monica."

Her fingers morphed into a shadowy dagger.

"Don't let your fear define you."

The foreigner sliced the ray gun out of Sissy's hand.

Val's eyes widened. She boosted forward and stopped in front of the bewildered Sissy. She immediately dug her right hand into the joker's stomach and launched her back across the rooftop.

Sissy rolled over and over until she came to a full stop. She laughed as she got up and looked at the pair.

"Whoa! Nice one! You really got me there!"

She sprang a laser rifle from her hand. She held it up and teased the trigger with her index finger. "But the fun isn't over yet!"

Val looked above the joker's head. "I'm not so sure about that."

The beast descended over Sissy and opened its gaping grin before she could notice. By the time she looked up, it was already too late.

"Uh-oh."

The nightmare chomped down on the redhead and swallowed her in one gulp.

Val looked away as someone else she knew disappeared from the universe forever.

Now wasn't the time for tears. She quickly grabbed little Monica and glided to the next rooftop. The monster licked its lips and cheerfully followed.

Val continued bounding from one building to the next, carefully paying attention to each blank edifice she landed on. Monica held on for dear life.

On the fifth building they soared to, Val noticed thin strands of shadow sprout from the rooftop's surface. They floated toward the sky and stopped growing at about seven feet. She blasted them with a surge of air, but the strings simply swayed like spaghetti.

One by one, each of the strands expanded its diameter. Circles bubbled on top of the cords and large white eye sockets rotated in odd positions along each sphere.

A revolting grin curled up on each of their faces. The colossal nightmare followed close behind the pair.

Val leaped onto the next building. A dozen shadowy figures already stood happily there, smiling at their guests upon arrival.

Val unzipped her coat and took out her liquor tin from an inside pocket. She peered behind her. The goliath already began illuminating their building.

She knew at that moment that they'd have no more rooftops to escape to. She crouched and set Monica down on the surface.

"Remember what I said before?"

Despite the pain, she forced a smile and placed her right hand on the girl's shoulder.

Monica shook the worried expression off her face and nodded. "Fear... doesn't define me."

"That's right." Val rose slowly. A current spiraled around her body. "Fear is all in our head."

The nightmare expanded its huge grin, preparing itself for its second meal of the day. Its grotesque head inched closer and closer.

"Do you trust me?"

The little girl took a step back, then nodded her head slowly.

"Good. Grab my hand." The girl placed her hand in Val's.

"Let's end this together."

The nightmare completely hung over them now. Val summoned as much wind as she could underneath her feet.

Just before the devil descended, Val and Monica flew straight into its mouth.

The pair spun in the monster's maw before they realized that a black hole sat below them. Monica panicked, her eyes wide open. Val reached over and grabbed the girl with her scorched hand. She held onto her more tightly than before.

"Remember what I said!" Val yelled above the roaring beast beneath them. "No more fear!"

Monica remembered and closed her eyes. Ink seeped into her skin once more. Once her body had completely darkened, Val knew she was ready. They breathed in together.

"Three!"

Breathed out.

"Two!"

Breathed in.

"One!"

Breathed out.

"Go!"

Val rocketed Monica straight toward the black hole. The little girl screamed as she stabbed two shadowy daggers into its eye.

The black hole exploded and swallowed the void. Nothingness consumed the universe and reset everything to zero.

Val woke up with her head against the bar counter.

Monica's nightmare was over.

She looked over and saw Sissy's dim-lit red ring resting at the bottom of a shot glass.

Priscilla was gone.

Val breathed in, breathed out. She reached over for the glass and popped out the ring before walking out of 'Barcade' in a hurry.

She ran to her bedroom when she arrived home. Her sheets lay scattered on the mattress.

Monica was nowhere to be found.

Chapter 14
Inner Demons

Val sat alone in a bar on a Tuesday night. The speakers blasted terrible alternative rock music as she downed her fifth Brave Bull.

For once, she had a quiet night to herself. Ice cubes clinked as she set her empty glass on the counter.

The airbender traced her index finger around the ring that lay in front of her. She had a lot to think about.

A young man pulled out a stool at the other end of the bar. He looked at the bartender and politely asked, "Orgasm, please."

Val glanced at her new companion. He didn't seem like the type that needed saving.

She looked down at the ring again. She saw a faint glimmer of herself there. The worn-out ceiling fan hummed in agreement overhead.

The bartender mixed some amaretto and rum. The young man took a peek at Val while waiting for his drink. She noticed, but didn't care.

One by one, Chrissy, Missy, Sissy and Silvia's faces flashed in her mind. A part of her wished they were all back in that weedy old shack on the outskirts of town. Then again, maybe that was just the alcohol.

She drank until the images washed away. If she thought of them for too long, she'd blame herself for everything that happened.

An Orgasm was neatly placed in front of the young man. Val waved for the bartender to come over.

"Another Brave Bull. Thanks."

Her newfound bar buddy snuck in another glance while sipping his juice. Val could feel his eyes, but continued to look down in front of her.

She grabbed the jewelry with her right thumb and index finger and spun it around on the counter. It danced before hitting a crack and falling abruptly.

"Hey."

The young man caught Val off-guard. She looked behind her.

"Do you mind if I sit here?" He pointed to the stool next to Val.

The windmaker didn't say a word. She returned to the ring on the counter.

The bartender swung back and placed a Brave Bull in front of Val. She gulped down a good amount immediately, getting ready to literally ghost her suitor at any moment.

The young man cleared his throat. He sounded too young to be in a shitty bar like this.

"I was wondering if I could ask you a question."

Val picked up the ring and spun it around again. She watched it bask in the dim light.

"What do you do for a living? I've noticed you here on weeknights before."

The ring fell off the counter and bounced on the floor below.

"Oh, I'll get it."

The boy got up and retrieved it. He placed it back in front of the motionless Val.

As he sat back down on his stool he said, "Sorry... I didn't mean to upset you."

Val stared forward, searching for an answer.

"I'll... I'll leave now." The gentleman got up off his seat. "Sorry for the—"

"Work," Val smirked. "I work for a living."

"Right." The young man awkwardly returned to the stool. "I guess that makes sense."

He waved over to the bartender and kindly asked, "Uh, another Orgasm, please."

Val looked at the man briefly before picking up the ring again. "Why do you order that?"

"Orgasm, you mean?"

She stared at her tiny reflection. "Yeah."

Her companion thought for a little bit before responding.

"It's sweet."

Val set the jewelry back down on the counter.

"I'm glad you think so."

The young man smiled. He folded his hands on the bar, then looked at Val's ring from the corner of his eye.

The bartender placed a fresh glass of Orgasm in front of him. The young man took a sip before asking the girl another question.

"So, if you don't mind me asking... what's with the ring?"

Val looked at her reflection again. "It's part of the job."

Her newfound friend nodded. "I see. So you're a jeweler or something?"

The airbender thought about the collection of rings she had at home. "Yeah, sort of."

"That's cool." The young man leaned forward. "Is there something special about that ring in particular?"

Val clasped her hand around her trinket. She felt its cold surface before slipping it into her jeans pocket.

"Nothing at all."

Her confidant sat back in his stool and returned to his drink. "Oh. I understand."

He gulped down the rest of his Orgasm and placed the empty glass on the counter. He turned to Val once more. She silently stared into her half-empty glass of Brave Bull. He could tell that something was on her mind.

"Excuse me for asking but… is something wrong?"

Val looked at her visitor with a sideways glance. The young man noticed his question annoyed her.

"You don't have to answer if you don't want to. I just thought…" The man traced his finger around the rim of his empty glass. "I just thought it was the right thing to ask. Sorry."

Val's annoyance faded. She looked ahead with a sad expression. "I just lost a friend."

The young man frowned and looked down at the bar. "I'm… I'm so sorry." He breathed in, breathed out. "Life isn't easy, no matter who you are." He shook around the ice in his glass. "I'm sorry that life is difficult for you right now."

Val nodded lightly and took a sip of her cocktail. "Yeah, me too."

Her visitor looked over at the dozens of clear, amber and orange bottles scattered across from him. "Sometimes it can be tough to put up with all the bullshit life brings." He folded his hands together. "But we can't let our inner demons take control."

Val dug her ring out from her jeans pocket and placed it on the counter again. She spun it around once more.

Her companion cleared his throat and summoned some courage to speak. "So, I was thinking, maybe we can talk some more if you're free later."

The jewelry spun to the edge of the bar. Val caught it before it fell and looked at her reflection one last time.

"I'll be busy then."

The young man turned away, slightly embarrassed. "Oh. I see." He scratched his head. "Is it work-related?"

Val smiled softly. "You wouldn't understand."

She slipped the ring onto her finger and vanished.

Chapter 15
The Morning After

A drizzle sprinkled down on the edge of a forest. A girl with long, white hair sat on a tree stump, looking down at the tall grass while gripping onto her scythe with two hands.

A roar reverberated through the sky. The girl tilted her head up and witnessed clouds directly above open in a circle. Two girls fell from the center.

The first snapped her hand back in midair. A deck of cards appeared between her index and middle fingers. She flung it forward fast.

The cards buried themselves in the grassy plain around the white-haired scythe girl. Each of them exploded. Large clouds of smoke billowed into the air.

When the smoke dissipated, goblins, ogres, trolls and dragons stood in the meadow, anxiously awaiting for their master to arrive.

The second falling girl aimed a bow in front of her and pulled its sting. She too unleashed an attack in midair, rocketing a single arrow downward.

The bolt duplicated into dozens of copies as it soared. They detonated upon contact, sending bits of dirt, bark and roots everywhere.

The scythe girl remained on her stump. Somehow, she knew she wasn't going to get hit.

The card girl touched down a few meters away in front of her monster collection. The bow girl followed shortly after. The former spawned another deck into her hand. The latter pulled back another arrow and aimed it at the white-haired specimen.

A fourth magical alcohol girl arrived from the woods behind her two colleagues. The wind kicked up as she entered the clearing. Her yellow raincoat danced.

She smiled as she spoke above the drizzle to the scythe girl across from her.

"Nice to meet you, Hailey."

ABOUT THE AUTHOR

David Lozada is a New York City-based writer with years of experience as a marketing professional, journalist and author. He has held a number of editorial positions online at such sites as Twinfinite, GameRevolution, DualShockers, Ranker and KeenGamer. David is one of the authors of The Future of Gaming and was the host of the KeenGamer Podcast.

David's passions include music, anime, cosplay, movies, bike riding and video games. This nerd is always out and about, going to anime and gaming conventions across America and posting all of his shenanigans on social media for the world to see. If you bump into him, wherever he may be, don't be shy to say hello!

Please visit www.davidjosephlozada.com, Twitter (@ZenoCreator125) or Instagram (@ZenoCreator125) for more information about David and his work.

www.ingramcontent.com/pod-product-compliance
Lightning Source LLC
Chambersburg PA
CBHW030742110726
47900CB00008B/2419